I0668273

REVERSED

WORLD

POWER

RYAN HODGE

SMP
PUBLISHING

SMP Publishing Edition

Printed in the United States of America

10 9 8 7 6 5 4 3 2 1

ISBN: 978-0997799002 (PBK)

DEDICATION

Dear Ma,

We'll always appreciate the love that you showered us with,
The love you blessed us with almost seems unreal-something like a myth.
I cherish boyhood memories holding your leg while walking down the Ave.,
All of the lessons of doing things the right way and all the things I can have.
You taught us how to be independent and strong,
You always promoted to never skip steps even if the process was long.
I remember every holiday we were five people deep,
Up playing cards and board games until we all fell asleep.
These are things we cherish and the times we'll always miss,
Because the love you poured on us was like being bathed in bliss.
We love you always and forever,
At the forefront of our minds, we'll forget you never.

Prologue

"Here come those blue-eyed devils. This is the moment I've been waiting for! On my cue I want you to open fire, but not a second before. We have to make sure they're all in our line of fire. We can't have any of them turn around and escape," I dictate.

"When do you want us to stop firing on them? Should we wait for your cue to cease firing too?" asks my friend.

"No, don't wait for my cue. You don't stop shooting until there's no more movement coming from them. You don't stop until they're all sent to hell. That's the only sign you'll need," I reply sternly.

We lie and wait for a few more minutes and allow them to get a little closer. Once they're closer, they'll be to the point of no return. This is a major step in attaining victory. It is crucial that we are victorious today.

"Get ready men! Get ready! Today's battle is not just for us, it's for our parents, our parents' parents, and our kids' kids. Almost there… Almost there… They're not going to know what hit them. Ready… Aim… Fire… Give them hell!" I order.

Gun fire erupts, decimating the silence and calm of the day. Gunshots bang through the air like fireworks over the Hudson River during Fourth of July celebrations. The fifty calibers we brought will take down these old wooden ships in no time. The smiles the white devils have on their faces suddenly turn to looks of horror. I bet those conniving bastards shit in their pants too. They thought today was going be sweet for them, but it's not. It's going to be sweet for us.

CHAPTER 1
Nayr's Perspective

The cop in the video says, "Get your ass on the ground nigger! Stop reaching for my gun. Don't move damn it. Don't fucking move! I'll shoot you dead in the street you black bastard."

The next thing we see is pure evil. The cop lets off seven shots hitting the guy with three of them. His lifeless body falls to the ground. We're dumbfounded by what we've just viewed.

"This is so damn foul! Not again. They keep killing unarmed black teens in the streets. He didn't deserve that," I say as I watch on.

Jay replies as he clenches his fist, "Damn it! He didn't even move. He complied with the officer's every command and the cop still shot him. What the hell!"

I remark, "That easily could've been one of us. Only thing he did wrong was have a blown license plate light bulb. They dragged him out of his car and shot him for that. This is some bullshit!"

"Well, it seems that being black in America is a crime. It always has been," states Jay.

Jay and I are seniors in high school and are ready to take the world by storm, but we are a bit apprehensive about the future because we see things getting worse around us daily. We're excited about college, but we can't get our minds past all of the unjust killings of innocent black men across the country. How can we truly focus on what we need to while we're terrified of being hunted down like animals in the wild? As we watch this video of yet another black person being killed on Facebook, we can't help but be angered and scared. You can be innocent and still be killed with no justice for you or your family.

My dad walks in with a friend as Jay and I watch the video on my phone. My dad who's a historian at heart and scientist by occupation overheard me curse as he walked into the living room. I know he's going to say something to me about my choice of words. He always does.

"Hello Nayr," my dad says.

"What's up Dad?" I ask.

My dad replies, "Nothing much son. Just trying to make an honest day's work. Good to see you Jay. This is Ken. He's a friend of mine, but he doesn't speak English. Just wave to him."

We wave to Mr. Ken and he waves back. My dad says something to Mr. Ken and then they turn to head to my dad's office.

"Good to see you too Mr. Smith. Can't wait to get back on the basketball court with you sir. You got lucky last time," Jay voices.

"Looking forward to it too, but it wasn't luck that I beat you. I beat you with strategy and brainpower. You're too young to understand that though," states my dad.

Jay responds, "You always say that sir, but I do use my brain and it never works."

"Jay, you said it right. Your brain never works. It never has and it never will," I reply jokingly.

"Oh you're roasting me! Good one Nayr! I'll get you back. You know I will," says Jay as he hits me with a throw pillow.

My dad speaks, "Yes, that was a good one son. You're very quick witted like your old man. I love to see you and other young people using your brains."

"Thanks Dad," I say as I raise my hand up to give him a fist bump.

Unfortunately, my dad doesn't raise his hand to meet my fist bump. I wonder why he didn't return my gesture. He just gave me kudos for being quick witted and then turns around and disses me. Jay gets his laughs back when he notices that my father left me hanging.

"Son, I see your look of befuddlement as to why I didn't meet your fist bump. I heard you using curse words when I initially walked in on you two. Now, I know you didn't know I was gonna come in at that moment, so I won't chastise you, but remember that you shouldn't use those vulgar terms. It makes you look like less of a man and makes you look quite uneducated," my dad lectures.

"Yes, I totally understand. I apologize. It won't happen again. I promise," I answer.

"That's good to know. I raised you better than that," quotes my dad. "Besides, the stuff in that phone of yours isn't that important or serious."

Jay states, "This time it is sir. What we were reacting to is extremely serious."

"I'm sure it was. Let me guess another fight video. Wait, I bet it was a half-naked girl popping her body parts around the camera," charges my dad.

I jump in, "Dad, it wasn't another twerk video or a fight video, but it was violent. It was so violent that it made me upset, so I used profanity to express my disapproval."

"Yeah, Mr. Smith. It's the same old violation of our rights as normal. I'm still upset about it and I was cursing too, but you just didn't hear me," Jay reports.

"I hate hearing about our civil rights being violated. Fellas, let me see what has you two so upset," says my dad.

I go back to my Facebook account to pull up the video. I want my dad to see why we're so angry. I'm sure he hasn't seen the video of this police shooting because that would have been the first thing he told us when he came through the door. He never takes those things lightly. Black people being murdered in the streets seem to always put him in a very reflective mood. I'm sure Jay and I will receive a very long lecture about this once my dad sees the footage.

The video loads up and my dad watches every second of it. He sees the young kid get shot by the cops three times and he wasn't even resisting. My dad chooses his words very carefully and doesn't speak without thinking. He always formulates his responses first and then speaks. My dad uses everything as a teachable moment. If there is a lesson to be learned from a situation, my dad will surely draw out the lesson and teach me. My dad plays the video back and scrutinizes it again. I see his brain muscles processing what to say. I can also tell that he disapproves of the senseless killing.

My dad speaks, "I can see why this video is upsetting to you two. This child is approximately your age and you feel like either of you could have been him lying there dead. This is a death that didn't have to happen and it's unfortunate. I'm saddened by it also."

"Dad, that's what we were just saying before you walked in. That guy the cop shot and killed was only 19 and was unarmed. It just doesn't make sense that he got killed like that," I say.

"I know you have a lot of questions about this and we will discuss them together, but I want to ask you two a couple of questions too," voices my father.

Jay asks, "What's that sir?"

"What could that young man have done differently to keep the situation from escalating?" inquires my dad.

"Well, I guess he shouldn't have argued with the cop to begin with. He did get pretty loud with the cop when he found out he got pulled over for a blown license plate light bulb," I reply.

"Also, the guy could have inspected his car to ensure he was compliant with the rules required to operate a vehicle legally," Jay words.

"You both make great points and you're correct in your responses. The officer was totally wrong in killing that young man and hopefully he'll be prosecuted to the fullest extent of the law. The young man also made a couple of mistakes during that traffic stop that unfortunately cost him his life," my pop says.

"What else did he do incorrectly?" I ask.

"He was wrong when he insulted the officer, refused to give the officer his registration, and didn't want to step out of the car when asked," my dad explains.

"Dad, I disagree with getting out of the car. He didn't do anything that warranted having to step out of the car," I say.

Jay chimes in, "I totally agree. His rights were being violated at the point when he was told to get out of the car. He hadn't done anything wrong."

"I see what you mean and I agree with you whole heartedly. That was a little overboard on the officer's actions. Now, let's get down to the nitty gritty of what happened," says Dad.

"Okay, let's go Dad. I wanna see how you flip this one to make sense," I reply.

Dad says, "No problem son. My mom used to tell me all the time whenever I would leave the house to be safe. No matter what I was doing she would always tell me to be safe."

"I don't get it Mr. Smith. We all know we should be safe. That's a no brainer. We do that all the time," Jays utters.

"What does it mean to you when someone tells you to be safe? Can you break it down for me?" inquires Dad.

"Yeah, it means to be careful, wear your seatbelt, and don't drink and drive," I verbalize.

Jay says, "It also means to be aware of your surroundings."

Jay and I 'dab' after we give our answers because we think we nailed it. My dad is not moved by our answers. He doesn't share the same enthusiasm that we have for our answers. Jay and I regain our focus and listen to what my dad has to say in response to our definitions.

"What my mom meant by being safe was all of those things you said and much more. It's really quite genius, but simple at the same time. Rule one of being safe is to never put yourself in jeopardy to be harmed. For example, you would never walk down a dark alley in D.C. Just like you shouldn't drink and drive because you could kill yourself or someone else. The young man put himself in harm's way by being disrespectful on the side of the road. Being safe, is about doing whatever it takes to make it home each night unharmed. Fellas, court cases are not fought on the side of the highway; they're litigated in a courtroom. His best bet would have been to comply with the officer's request, make it home safely, and then file a grievance with the courts later," my dad narrates.

"So, basically the strategy is to live to fight another day?" I ask.

"Son, that's exactly what I'm saying. Remember this guys, anything you do on the side of the road that is defiant will give the cop a reason to harm you and possibly get off with no charges. You being dead on the side of the road doesn't help me, doesn't help Jay's parents or anyone else. It's all about using a strategy to get yourself out of a sticky situation, but never escalate a situation with a cop. It may end up being your last day if you do," Dad remarks.

"Thanks Mr. Smith. That makes a lot of sense. I know my parents would rather me make it home safely and be able to talk to them about whatever happened as opposed to planning my funeral," Jay utters.

"That's my point. Get home safely and live to let your voice be heard. I'd rather boycott and protest alongside of you living than alone with you dead. You're putting yourself in great risk by resisting at 2 a.m. on a dark road with three white cops pulling you over. Think about your chances of coming out of that situation on top," orates Dad.

"Dad, we get it now. Don't put yourself in a bad spot to be harmed whether it's by the cops, a gang, or even a girlfriend," I acknowledge.

"Well said son. One more thing and then I'll let you two continue without me. Just because you're mad about something really isn't a justification for losing your cool. Even in times of tragedy you need to be level headed and with clear thought. That is the only way to bring calm to the situation. Chances are if you're emotional, you will do things without thinking them through," Dad speaks.

"One more thing Dad," I say.

Dad responds, "Anything son. Shoot."

"What about the people who fully comply with every request they make and they still get murdered? How do we circumvent that?" I ask.

Dad answers, "Well, son we have to change the mindset of the people pulling us over. When they view our lives as being as important as theirs, the problem will no longer exist. Don't worry guys because change is coming."

My dad walks to his office to join his colleague and leaves me and Jay to our social media surfing. Jay and I have a new perspective on how to proceed with our interactions with the police and other people in general. I think we'll be better off going forward because of the conversation we had with my dad.

"Man, your dad has an answer for everything. I know you don't win any arguments with him," Jay comments.

I respond, "Jay, I never argue with him. There's no point because I won't win. It would be a total waste of time."

We laugh and eventually look at more videos online. We see other videos that are funny and they cheer us up a little bit. In the back of our heads, we know that we could be killed on the side of the road.

I say, "These videos are crazy and unpredictable."

Jay jokes, "What's unpredictable is the people your dad always brings around. They always look funny."

"You always use that joke. It's time for a new one. Besides, you know my dad is a scientist who loves languages, history, and all that boring stuff. It's just his thing. You know he's the department head at Seton Hall University. He's even taught me some of that stuff, even though I don't know it perfectly," I explain.

CHAPTER 2
Harry's Perspective

"Quiet down students. What do you know about quantum mechanics?" I inquire to my class.

One student responds, "I know it's also called quantum physics or theory."

"That's absolutely correct, but that's surface information. That doesn't tell us much about what quantum mechanics is. Someone delves deeper into what it is," I respond.

"I know it deals with the work of Max Planck. From what I remember it pertains to the processes of atoms and photons," another student answers.

I say, "Now we're getting somewhere. Keep in mind that Albert Einstein offered a quantum based theory to explain the photoelectric effect."

I lecture the class on the particulars of Einstein's theory and Planck's work. They ask many questions throughout the lecture, for this topic is quite confusing and intricate. Many students question the results of Einstein and Planck. I love when students challenge science. That's one of my purposes of being their professor.

I want to influence my students to challenge what's been theorized and break ground of their own. In my classes, I want them to reinvent the wheel because the product they produce may be better than the wheel itself. Without forward and progressive thought, the world would exist as it did generations ago. I teach my son and my students to always push the envelope. Why be good when you can be great?

"Okay students, don't forget to turn in your papers electronically by 11:59 tonight, otherwise they're late. For those of you who opted to do the project on the structure of the atom, be sure to turn them in to my office before five o'clock today. My assistant will be there until five to collect them. If there are no more questions or concerns for me, class is dismissed. Today was a great class," I speak.

I love it when our class discussions are filled with many insightful comments. It makes me feel like I'm earning my paycheck when students actually do their assignments at home and come to class prepared to work. Information being processed and disseminated always gives me a high. I got so engulfed in today's class discussion that I almost forgot that I need to leave campus early to attend a conference of geologists and geographers. Geology and geography are out of my field of study, but I want to attend the conference nonetheless. I think the conference will be entertaining and if it's not entertaining it'll at least be informative. There's no such thing as bad or useless information.

I pack up my briefcase and walk to my car. I'm in a great mood and I'm getting off campus before traffic gets ridiculous and gets deadlocked. I whisk home in record time. It normally takes me forty five minutes to get back home to Linden, but not today. It only takes me thirty minutes to arrive home. I love being ahead of the game. Now, I have time to eat something at the house instead of on the go.

When I walk into the house, I hear several people shouting from the game room upstairs. My first thought is that Nayr and his buddies are up there playing video games, but after a more refined listen, I realize that those are shouts of anger and frustration. Now, I know those boys aren't fighting. What could cause them to get into a physical altercation in here? They normally get along so well.

I rush upstairs to the game room and don't see anything immediately aloof. Some of the boys are sitting and some are standing while they watch television. Something on the tube has garnered their attention and infuriated them. The boys are watching the news. Now, I know something is wrong if a room full of teenage boys is watching the news instead of videos or something more entertainment based.

"Nayr, what's going on? What's all of the commotion about?" I inquire.

"I'm sorry Dad, but we were watching the latest video released and the guys were upset. I promise I wasn't yelling like last time. I understand your point about not losing my cool every time I see something or hear something upsetting," Nayr responds.

"I'm glad you're not upset son. Thanks for listening to my suggestions, but I don't see what video you speak of," I verbalize.

"Mr. Smith, it's another video showing the cops killing another black kid. They shot him dead on sight," Jay reports.

"Dad, just wait. I'm sure they'll play it again. They've been playing it back to back for the last half hour. I think they just released it to the media," Nayr says.

The news station comes back from commercial, but they aren't playing the video. Instead, they're interviewing someone who's close to the case. I just want to see the video. I know it's circulating online by now. One of these young men can find it.

I ask, "Can one of you pull the video up online? Has no one sent you the video on your phone?"

Within seconds, Jay has the video up on his phone and I'm watching it, but it's too small to clearly see what's going on. The boys have no problem seeing the video on Jay's phone and poke fun at me about losing my eyesight. I guess my eyes aren't what they used to be. Fortunately, the video of the shooting is being broadcasted on the television again. The boy who was shot isn't even a teenager. He was only twelve years old. This is hard to watch to say the least. I see why the boys are shaken again. The cops pulled up to the scene and killed that boy in less than five seconds. It's almost like the cops decided before they got there that they were going to kill that kid. Man, this is almost like premeditated murder. They could have exhausted other options before they decided that boy had to die.

"Guys, we just had a similar conversation like this not too long ago. It's unfortunate that we keep talking about the same acts of violence against black people. It has to stop now and it will," I narrate.

"Dad, do you think the cops will get in trouble for this act of violence? Why do they just keep gunning black people down like this?" Nayr asks.

Jay replies, "It's because they can. Nothing ever happens to them when they harm us. Somehow it ends up being our fault. Black lives don't matter to them."

"It's sad to say, but I don't think they'll be charged or convicted. It's just the way things are and how they've always been. That's why it's important to protect yourselves and be safe at all times. Don't give the police as they'll call it, the justifiable reason to shoot you because the law is on their side," I orate.

I hate that I have to get to this conference at a time like now, but it's necessary that I go. I've schooled my son on this very topic over and over again, so he'll be able to cope through this until I return. The boy who held that fake gun didn't have to die like that. He should be home right now playing as little kids play. Someone needs to be held accountable for what transpired in that video.

"Guys, before I go, I want to tell you something. I don't seek to infuriate you by telling you this or to make you afraid. My point in what I'm going to tell you is to make you aware of where you live and the circumstances we live in. Remember this: This country was not designed for the black man to prosper. We were considered the lowest of the low and were property to be discarded of, abused, and sold at the whim of another person. When the laws of this land were created, we were not intended to benefit from them. Now, it's hundreds of years later and we still don't have equality. As you move about in your day to day activities, be mindful that this country was built on the backbones of our ancestors and you're a minority. We are still the oppressed, but we will not always be the oppressed," I vocalize. "The system was not designed by us or for us, so don't expect for it to be equal."

After that, Nayr's friends leave the house. I grab my suitcase for the trip. I'm glad I was able to get home early because that gave me a chance to talk to my son and his friends about the shooting. It's all over the news and social media. These kids are constantly bombarded with these injustices and need people to work through these atrocities with them. As I load the car with my luggage, I tell Nayr to help me. While we load the trunk, we continue to converse.

"Dad, sometimes I just wanna grab one of the guns we go hunting or to the range with and keep it with me for protection against the police. It seems like it's the only way to protect myself from them," comments Nayr.

"Son, I'm sorry you feel like you have to protect yourself from the police. I don't like that you fear them, but I totally understand you. Arming yourself to engage the police is a bad idea because they will shoot you dead in an instance. Arm yourself with your mind. That's the best advice I can give you. If you use your mind the way I've trained you to do, you'll beat the cops without ever using a weapon," I voice.

"I use my mind Dad as you've instilled in me to do, but it's just frustrating seeing how meaningless our lives appear to be to them. I don't like feeling like this. I just want a fair shake out of life and I don't want it cut short because I have a broken tail light," says Nayr.

"Son, it won't be. You'll get yours even if you have to work a little harder and go above and beyond to get it. Don't be discouraged," I say.

"Thanks Dad. I will stay the course and not falter," my son replies. "I'm glad you're here to help me work through this."

"Son, do you still have your quick bag packed?" I ask.

"I always have that bag packed. I got tired of you getting at me for not having it ready to go. It's in my room in the closet right where you told me to put it," utters Nayr.

I tell Nayr to grab his bag because he's coming with me to this conference. I think we need this time to talk. He still has questions that I need to answer. The last thing I need is for something to bother him while I'm gone and he not handle it the right way. I'd never forgive myself if he got into some mischief because he couldn't access me. The conference may be beneficial to him. This conference may spark something inside of him that he may use in his future.

He runs inside and grabs his bag. He's back to the car in no time. I look forward to the time with my son. We haven't had this one on one time since we went hunting a few months ago. I must say that he is a pretty good shot. He now shows me things about guns and tactics. Nayr even has had us enter paintball competitions and we've won first place on two separate occasions. It always amazes me how sometimes the teacher has becomes the pupil. We drive to D.C. and check into the hotel. My son has school tomorrow, but this father-son time is more beneficial to him in my opinion. I inform him that he has to take notes on the conference. He doesn't mind because he'd rather be with me out of town than to be at school. Nayr and I talk a little bit more after we check into the hotel and then I turn in for the night.

CHAPTER 3
Harry's Perspective

We wake up the next morning and shower up. The hotel we're in is magnificent. I'll be sure to stay here the next time I visit our nation's capital. After we hit the shower, we head downstairs to eat breakfast. The conference is at Georgetown University, so we head over to the campus. The campus is beautiful and has great architecture. They really put a lot of work into the beautification of this campus.

We arrive in the auditorium where the conference is being held about fifteen minutes before the conference begins. Nayr and I meet a few of the presenters for today's conference. Many of the presenters ask me what field of study I'm in. Most of them assume that I'm a geologist or geographer, but I'm not. They are very surprised when I tell them that I'm a Particle

Physicist. I'm just a nerd like that. The presenters figure that I'll be bored or not quite get the gist of their findings.

I like to consider myself a fairly intelligent man, so I think I'll be fine at this conference. I doubt that any of this information will go over my head. Nayr will benefit from this educationally too. He'll be able to bring some of this information back to his school and maybe share it or use it on a test. You never know. We sit up front, so I can take in as much information as possible. I don't want to miss anything.

The presenters here today are supposed to be the preeminent geologists and geographers in the world. I'm sure they have tons of information about the world as it exists today and in the past. You have to understand where you came from and where you're at, to know where you're going. The conference starts right at nine o'clock as it is scheduled. I'm glad it starts on time because I abhor tardiness.

The presenters provide a variety of information. Some presenters discuss minerals found in certain regions of the world, others discuss earthquakes and landslides, while others discuss methods to extract minerals from the earth. All of those presenters do a great job of getting their points across, but I'm really interested in the presenter who will discuss tectonic plate movements. Dr. Robinson discusses how tectonic plates have shifted from centuries ago. She even has a digital model of how the continental drift occurred.

It fascinates me how the world was once all connected to each other and now it's not. Basically, it can all be blamed on earthquakes to simplify it. I couldn't imagine being able to drive to Africa. The concept of that seems foreign, but at one point it was possible to get to Africa without having to sail across a huge body of water.

"Son, how'd you like the model of the way the world became what it is today?" I ask.

"Dad, I thought it was pretty cool. I'd never seen a realistic model like the one Dr. Robinson showed us. The depictions from school didn't do a great job of showing the transformation so vividly. I'm thoroughly impressed," says Nayr.

"I agree. I thought that was pretty nice too. I also liked the way she broke it down from prehistoric times all the way through times of slavery and up until current times. That was great!" I reply.

"I always wanted to live in California, but I don't know about that now Dad. Chances are, California will one day be in the Pacific Ocean and not connected to the Continental United States. I don't wanna find myself floating away one night," jokes Nayr.

We both laugh at Nayr's joke. My son is quite witty and I'm proud of him and his accomplishments. He's been through a lot since his mom passed away, but he's handled the adversity like a soldier. He didn't use his mother's death as a scapegoat to fall off track.

There's a short intermission in between Dr. Robinson's presentation and the next presenter. Fortunately, my son and I are in the front and I'm able to get to Dr. Robinson first. I have a few questions to ask her about her work. I introduce myself and my son and she smiles and greets us in return.

"Can your research be found online anywhere?" I ask.

She gives me her business card with all of her contact information on it as well as her website address. I will be sure to go to her site to see what all is on there. I'm sure it's filled with a lot of useful information. This is why I attend events such as this because there is so much to learn if you step out of your comfort zone or area of expertise.

"Can I ask you one more question before I let you go?" I ask.

"That's your one question right there," Dr. Robinson jokes. "Of course you can ask another question. That's what I'm here for."

"You spoke of continental drift in your presentation. I was wondering at what rate do land masses move during an average year," I say.

"Great question. Based on my research over the last thirty years, earth's land masses move toward and away from one another about .6

inches per year. That's a pretty specific question. I don't normally get questions like that," Dr. Robinson replies.

"I just like to be detailed is all. I try to teach my son to be detailed, so I have to lead by example. He needs to see these types of conversations, so he knows the right questions to ask," I speak.

"I understand. He's lucky to have a father like you on his side. I'm sure his mother is proud to have you by her side," Dr. Robinson remarks.

"Thanks! He seems to appreciate having his old man around. He's a very well-mannered young man. And his mother, God rest her soul, showed her appreciation for me daily. We miss her, but we're managing," I report.

"Sorry to hear that. I know that's tough to deal with. A death of a loved one can be a devastating blow. I'm sorry you had to go through that. I'm glad to see you two are prospering even in the face of hardships," Dr. Robinson states. "Let me give you my personal number. It's not on my card."

I put her personal contact information in my phone immediately. I'm not normally impressed by people during my first visit, but this time I am. She's intelligent, well spoken, and gorgeous. She's a keeper. My son and I decide to skip the next session and head to the car to go grab some lunch from a deli around the corner from the campus. We converse while we ride.

"Dad, I think Dr. Robinson likes you. I bet you nobody else will get her personal phone number. I hope you call her when we get back to Linden. My dad has the juice. Wait until I tell my boys that you snagged a dime," comments Nayr.

I downplay my attraction to Dr. Robinson. He doesn't need to know that I find her ravishing. I don't want anything throwing him off track. His future is the most important thing to me.

"Son, you know I have to focus on you and making sure you're straight. You need me and I won't let you down. You're the most important person in my life," I say.

"Come on Dad. I know you like her. Shoot, I'm only 18 and I like her. You don't have to keep shying away from women for me. I'm good. I know you need female companionship. You haven't had a woman around since mom died. It's time Dad. It's time for you to live a little. Besides, I'll be graduating soon and will be out of the house. It'll be good for you to have a little something to spend some time with," utters my son.

"I love you son and the last thing I want is for you to think someone else comes before you. If you say it's okay, I might just give the good ole doc a call," I respond.

"I know you love me and I love you too. You show me that every day, but it's time you show someone else who deserves you some love. Dr. Robinson may be the one," observes Nayr.

My son is so insightful. He's the perfect blend of his mother and me. I wish she were still alive to see the handsome and responsible son she always hoped he'd be. She'd be just as proud of him as I am today. I guess we did something right.

"Alright, I'll give her a call sometime next week. I'm not going to lie, she's definitely a looker. I could tell she was into me too. I saw the way she was looking into my dreamy brown eyes," I remark.

Nayr states, "Yeah, she sure was on you the entire time you two talked. She couldn't take her eyes off of you. Make sure you find out if she has a daughter."

"Son, you are too much. Calm your hormones," I shoot back.

"Oh no Dad, it's nothing like that. I just want to start networking before I go to college. If she has a daughter, she's probably real smart. I can benefit from having intelligent friends. You tell me all the time to keep determined people in close council," Nayr verbalizes.

"Son, feed that garbage to someone else. I know better. Don't forget that I was your age at one point," I say.

Nayr and I eat lunch. After we eat, we go back to the conference to finish the afternoon. We gain more useful information, but nothing quite as informative as Dr. Robinson's lecture. I do believe that I hit a homerun today with her. The conference ends and we get back on the road to head home. Today was great. I learned valuable information, I got to spend time with my son, and I met a beautiful lady. I can't deny that I'm winning right now.

CHAPTER 4
Nayr's Perspective

It's been a while since my dad and I went to the conference in Washington D.C. My dad has been working in the basement a lot since we came back. It's safe to say that Dr. Robinson sparked something inside of him. I haven't seen the fire inside of him lit like this since he converted the basement into his personal laboratory. I'm extremely delighted that I went to the conference with him because had I not, he probably wouldn't have said anything to the doctor.

Dr. Robinson and my dad have talked every day, since their initial meeting. My dad seems happier these days and I know it's because of his new relationship. The best part about it is that my dad has less time to worry about what I'm doing because he's preoccupied with his work and Dr. Robinson. My dad even told me that Dr.

Robinson will be visiting soon. I'm still kind of shocked that my dad is entertaining a love interest and I'm even more surprised that he's going to bring her here. It's cool with me because he needs a woman desperately.

I don't have time to hang around my dad. Not that he isn't cool, but I graduate this year and I don't have time to tend to my dad and his affairs. I have to attend to things related to what teenagers do. I have to get ready for Linden High School's senior prom, then the Senior Banquet, and then the Senior Bash. At least I don't have to worry about my college paperwork because it's already done.

I had three full academic scholarships offered to me from Temple, Howard, and Seton Hall Universities. I accepted the full ride to Howard University because I wanted to be near home, but far enough that it wouldn't seem like I never left. Tonight, I have some teenager related business to handle. My boy Jay is celebrating his 18th birthday at a fancy ballroom in Bridgewater. Everybody's going to be there and I'm not missing it. Besides, Jay is my man one hundred grand, so I am honored to be there. His parents are going all out for this party. Jay is going to be like a king at his party and I'll be like a prince. I can't wait to get there and turn up. The party will definitely be lit!

I'm in my room getting dressed for the party. I see some lights shine through my window, so I look outside. I see my dad pulling into the driveway. He's normally home much earlier than now. I guess he worked late at the university. It would make sense if he worked late because the semester is coming to an end. He enters the house and comes upstairs.

"Son, turn that music down. Your hearing will be gone in the next ten years if you keep listening to music at that volume. I really don't see how you take it. All that blaring is too much for me," my dad speaks.

"Dad, the music isn't that loud, but the reason you can't stand it is because you're old," I say jokingly.

"Don't think your old man doesn't still have a little something left in the tank because I do. You shouldn't underestimate me son. You really shouldn't underestimate any foe or situation. It isn't prudent to do that," Dad explains. "The underestimating will be what has you defeated. Always remember that."

"I will," I say.

My dad begins to dance to the music I have playing. I don't tell him, but he's actually pretty light on his feet for an old guy. My dad probably looks ten years younger than he actually is. He doesn't pollute his body with anything. He doesn't drink alcohol or smoke. He barely even drinks soda. I try to model myself after him as much as possible because what he does works. He provides for me and doesn't take shortcuts. I would be happy to be his age and still look as good as he does. In fact, many people who don't know him think he's my older brother.

"Dad, please stop dancing. You may hurt yourself. You know you have old bones and I don't want them to crack. I wouldn't be able to explain you falling into pieces to the emergency responders who come to get you," I remark.

"That's funny. I'll be sure not to tell your friends who won the last basketball game we played. I'm sure they would clown you for letting someone as ancient as me beat you on the court. But don't get off the subject, turn that music down," Dad words.

I voice, "No, you don't need to mention that. We agreed that's our little secret. The fellas don't need to know anything about that. Plus, you know my knee was sore that day."

"Sure it was. Looks like you're ready for the party. New shoes, new hat, and a new shirt. I must be giving you too much allowance money," Dad speculates.

"I'm ready for sure Dad. Me and the fellas will be the life of the party and you give me enough allowance, but not too much. I just manage what you give me well," I utter.

"That's good you manage it well. Managing your money is part of being a man. Son, any fool can be reckless, but not everyone is responsible. I'm glad you choose to be responsible. I'm proud of you son. Well, I'm going to shower and get some rest. You know it's a school night, so don't party too hard. I'm only letting you go because it's Jay's party and tell him happy birthday for me," Dad emphasizes.

"Good night Dad. I'll see you in the morning for breakfast, unless you're too tired to get out of bed. I'll party hard, but it will be responsibly hard," I verbalize.

"That's good enough for me. Good night son. And I'll be ready for breakfast before you, jokester," my dad shoots back.

My dad walks to his room and I finish getting dressed. My phone is blowing up with messages about the party tonight. Everybody's excited about it. I take some selfies in the mirror and post them to Instagram and Snapchat. My accounts are going crazy. I know that I'm looking good and they know it too. My outfit is lit and I'm lit, so it's time to go. I walk past my dad's room and shout out to him that I'm leaving to head to the party.

"What's the number one rule for the night?" asks dad.

"Dad, you know I know. We've been through this a thousand times before," I reply.

"So, tell me what it is and then you can go about your business," Dad shouts from the shower.

"The number one rule is to be safe. It's probably imprinted on my brain. Not probably, definitely," I respond.

"Great! Now, you can get out and let me get back to my shower," Dad orders.

I exit the house and jump in my car. The drive from Linden to Bridgewater is about 45 minutes long and I'm taking the drive solo. I drive by myself to keep from having drama from the people riding with me. It seems like every time I ride with my peers, things never go the way they're supposed to go. As I'm leaving my block to head to the party, I get a phone call from one of my boys.

"What's up bruh?" I ask.

"Nothing. I'm trying to hit the party up, but I have a flat tire. I tried to put air in it, but it didn't take," Josh says.

"Damn, that's wack. You know how things go when it's time to go somewhere. That tire waited until the last minute to go out on you. It's life," I reply.

Josh asks, "Where are you? Can you come get me?"

"Man, I'm already in route to the party. You know I'm always on time for everything. Can't be late to Jay's party. You know I'm like the guest of honor," I state.

"Nayr, you know I'm always on time too. I didn't expect the car to put me down. I'm ready to roll now. Come on. Don't leave me hanging. Come scoop your boy," Josh urges.

"Alright, but you better be ready when I get there. I'm just pulling up and you gotta be ready to jump in the car. I'm barely gonna stop the car," I report.

Josh agrees to be ready as soon as I pull up to his house. For that reason, I decide to go pick him up. About five minutes, later I pull up to Josh's house and he's outside waiting for me. We leave immediately and head to Route 22 for the party. Josh and I drive to the party with the top to the Camaro down. The night is beautiful and the weather is very comfortable. The entire time we ride to the party we discuss how lit the party is going to be and how we're going to have tons of fun.

"Shit!" I blurt out as I look in the rear view mirror.

"What's wrong Nayr? What do you see?" asks Josh.

"A police officer is behind us. We didn't do anything. I wasn't speeding, so we should be good and we both have on our seatbelts. This car is brand new and has nothing wrong with it," I speak.

"Well, something has to be wrong otherwise he wouldn't be behind us. I'm shook because you know how cops like to do innocent black men," Josh comments. "And he just put on his blue lights."

"I wanna pull over, but this isn't a safe place to do so. And the car next to us isn't moving out of the way, so I just have to hold the lane a little longer," I utter.

"I know that cop is going to be livid at us for not pulling over. Maybe you should stop right here in the lane. The cops already be angry at us, so we don't want to piss them off even more," Josh orates.

"I understand your point of view, but we can't just stop in the middle of a driving lane. I don't care about the cop, but we could be killed. I'm not trying to die at age 18 during a traffic stop. No way, bruh," I communicate.

Finally, I have the opportunity to get over to the shoulder so we can see why we're being stopped. As soon as I get over one lane, the cop goes flying past me and doesn't even look our way. Clearly, we aren't who he's after. I'm glad we didn't panic because he could have flipped on us. Josh calms down and we continue riding to the party. That's enough suspense for me for the rest of the night.

We arrive at the party before anybody starts dancing. Jay is going to arrive late on purpose, so he can make a grand entrance. He has a penchant for dramatic entrances. I like dramatics also, but I like dramatic performances, so I'll shine on the dance floor. I hit the bathroom to check myself over thoroughly. I'm good to go, so I exit the bathroom and beeline straight to the dance floor because I hear a song that I like. I have no problem starting the party. I live for these types of moments.

About forty-five minutes into the party, Jay arrives in a limousine. His parents have a huge red carpet rolled into the ballroom. Jay enters the party as if he's on the red carpet at a celebrity event. His parents have arranged for his favorite song to be playing as he walks in. Jay goes straight to the dance floor and begins dancing. We all crowd around him and give him props. At that moment, the party spiked to a higher energy and excitement level and it doesn't subside for the duration of the night. For the rest of the night we Whip, Dab, and do other dances to the music.

The night is filled with many laughs and great memories. Unfortunately, the night ends in a blink of an eye. I can't complain because I had a great time and thoroughly enjoyed myself. My shirt is drenched with sweat and I'm sure I lost five pounds tonight. Everybody's filing out of the party heading to their cars.

"Nayr, Nayr," one of my classmates calls.

There are so many people out here and it's so dark that I can't see who's calling me. Next, I feel a hand caressing my back. When I look over my shoulder, I see a pleasant face staring at me. I'm so glad it's her. We danced together for at least five songs tonight. I knew she was feeling me from the way she was twerking on me.

"What's up Kelsey?" I ask.

"You tell me. I know you not trying to go home without me," Kelsey says.

I respond, "No, I'm not. I was looking for you when I heard you calling my name. I can't see anything out here though."

"Oh okay. Well, I'm getting in with you. Me and Ashley got dropped off, so you can take us back to Linden and then me and you can hook up," Kelsey reports.

"Josh rode with me here, but it's no problem that we ride back together. In fact, see if Ashley wants to hook up with Josh," I suggest.

Kelsey goes to see if Ashley wants to hook up with Josh. I find Josh in the parking lot, so I can tell him what's going on. He's all for hooking up with Ashley. I knew he'd be interested in her because he talked about her earlier. Minutes later, Kelsey and Ashley return and tell us they're ready to leave with us. Josh is good and so am I, so we jump in the car with the girls and start driving back to Linden.

During the ride back to Linden, we have the music playing and are having a good time. The girls' hair is blowing in the wind as we drive down Route 22. The night is ours and we can't wait to get back to Linden.

"Damn! Not again. Another damn cop is behind us again," I report.

"Well, it's just like on the way here. Maybe you just need to get out of the cop's way and we'll be fine," says Josh.

The girls jerk their heads to look at the cop as he drives behind us. I'm a little upset that they turned and looked at him because it may seem suspicious to the police. I don't panic because we haven't done anything wrong and they may not be pulling us over. I'm clear to get over a lane, so I do so. The cop throws on his blue lights and gets behind me again. Obviously, he is pulling us over. Therefore, I get over one more lane and pull to the shoulder. We are all nervous now.

The cop gets out of his car and walks up to mine. He requests my insurance card, license, and registration and I oblige. I'm wondering why he pulled us over, but I'll wait to see if he offers a reason as to why. The cop comes back to the car and tells me and Josh to step out of the car. I'm confused as to why we need to get out of the car, but I comply. Josh is angered by the police officer's request.

"Why do I need to get out of the car officer? You do know I wasn't driving? Since when does a non-driver have to exit a car being pulled over?" Josh questions angrily.

"I don't have to answer your questions boy! Just get out the car like I told you to. That's a direct order," asserts the cop.

I'm out of the car while the cop yells at Josh. The cop tells Josh either he'll get out of the car on his own or he will make Josh exit the car. Two minutes later, two more squad cars pull up. The cop who initially pulled us over slammed me to the ground and cuffed me as the other two cops approach Josh on the passenger's side of my car. Josh becomes more upset when he sees me get thrown to the ground.

Kelsey and Ashley are recording the entire episode. They can't believe what they are seeing. They keep screaming for the cop to leave me alone and that I didn't do anything. When the cops get close to Josh's door he speaks.

"This is bullshit! You pigs are only pulling us over because we are two black guys in a nice car with two white girls. I'm sure it was killing you when you saw them in the car with us. I bet you pictured them being your daughters. Racist pigs!" Josh rants.

"Last chance for you buddy. Get out of the car," one cop orders.

Finally, Josh gives up. He puts his hands straight up in the air after he opens the door. What Josh does next surprises me. After he opens the door, he lies flat on the ground. The two police officers immediately pounce on him. You would think that he was resisting arrest the way they begin pummeling him. They ask Josh his name as they hit him, but he doesn't tell them. Next, the cop who slammed me to the ground asks me Josh's name.

"What's his fucking name boy?" he asks.

I don't answer because my face is mashed into the ground. I can barely breathe let alone speak. Josh screams while the cops beat him for nothing. I even hear Josh scream that he can't breathe. The cop gets more angry when I don't answer him even though he is the reason why I can't answer. He begins to knee me over and over in my rib cage as he holds my face to the ground. Josh's screams about not being able to breathe go silent. I no longer hear anything from him. The girls are crying uncontrollably and I fear for the worst.

The two cops who were assaulting Josh are now calling for an ambulance. The cop finally stops kneeing me in the ribs when he realizes what has happened. The cop stands me up against the car on the passenger's side. Josh's bloody and lifeless body lies on the side of the highway. Man, this is a nightmare. The ambulance pulls up and they put Josh on a stretcher and put him inside. The cop gives me my paperwork back and tells us to go home. I was not cited and I still don't know why we were stopped to begin with. We drive back to Linden and I drop Ashley and Kelsey home. Kelsey sends me the video of Josh's murder as I drive away. Josh's family needs to know what happened tonight, so before I head home, I stop by his parents' house. I would hate for them to find out what transpired tonight from social media or the news. Josh's family is hurt and enraged by his death and leave the house immediately to begin to get answers to his senseless death. I drive home with extremely sore and bruised ribs and scratches on my face and hands. I'm in pain, but I know I don't need medical attention.

CHAPTER 5
Nayr's Perspective

I know my dad is going to be out of this world upset when I tell him what transpired tonight. He's going to be upset to the point that I don't want to tell him. I hate disappointing my dad, that's why I always strive to do my best. I know tonight's happenings weren't my fault, but it still happened to me and it will upset my dad. I think my dad will be even more upset that I did nothing wrong and was still victimized. He has always been highly critical of the police ever since the civil rights movement.

When my granddad was alive, he marched with Dr. King and my dad was able to meet him. My father doesn't remember much about him because he was only four years old at the time. Dr. Martin Luther King Jr. was assassinated a year later, but my grandfather worked hand in hand with Dr. King and helped organize the Alabama Bus Boycott. Even after Dr. King died, my dad was often around when Civil Rights Activists had rallies and he even has pictures to prove it. Even though my dad was young, he has the scars from when the white cops turned loose the K-9 unit on non-violent protesters. He tells me the story all the time of how afraid he was, but my grandfather believed this path was necessary to bring about change.

Unfortunately, my grandfather was killed prematurely like Dr. King was. My granddad was murdered by some unlawful cops who pulled him and my dad over one night in Georgia after a Civil Rights rally. My dad witnessed the entire thing and by the grace of God survived the attack. They beat him too and left him for dead, but a passerby from the rally picked him up and ultimately saved his life. My father never could come to terms with what happened to him and his dad, but vowed to work tirelessly to prevent it from happening to me. Unfortunately, I was victimized tonight and my dad will somehow make it his fault.

I walk to my dad's room to tell him what went down. The walk to his room seems to take an hour and a half. I get in front of his door and take a deep breath. I knock lightly in hopes that he won't hear me and I'll just go to sleep. To my surprise, my dad hears my faint knock.

"Son, come in. I'm awake," Dad voices.

I enter my dad's room. He's resting in bed doing some reading. I know he was only waiting for me to get home safely. He never sleeps well or doesn't sleep at all when I'm not home. I guess that's a parental curse or something. It's like he can't fully rest comfortably unless I'm home.

"How was the party? Did you have a good time?" he asks.

I answer, "The party was great! Was the best one I've been to. We partied all night long. The DJ played nonstop hits. It was a lot of fun."

"Well, that's great son. I'm glad you had a great time. Must have been pretty good to be considered the best party you've ever been to. It's a special thing when young people can hang out with each other and not have any conflict. You know your generation is filled with wanna be tough guys," Dad orates.

"Yeah, I agree. A lot of guys are ratchet and wanna be gangsters. We had no drama at the party. Everyone was well behaved," I speak.

"Son, you specifically said that there was no drama at the party. Was there drama with any other part of the night?" Dad inquires.

"Yes, Dad. Unfortunately, there was immense drama after the party. Everything was going along just great and then the night turned nightmarish in the blink of an eye," I utter.

My dad tells me to turn on the room light and he turns off his reading light. He sees my dirty clothes and slightly scratched up face as he gets out of bed. His face is one of confusion, rage, and hurt, but he doesn't say anything initially. His demeanor is calm and calculated like it always is. My dad never loses his composure. The first thing he does is give me a hug.

"I'm glad you're okay son. Meet me downstairs in the kitchen, so you can bring me up to speed on what materialized tonight," Dad words.

I head downstairs to the kitchen and wait for my dad to come talk to me. I don't know if I should start from the very beginning of the night or just from the point when we got stopped by the police. I don't know if I can tell the story without losing my cool, so I have to figure something else out. My dad finally makes it to the kitchen and has a cloth to clean my face with. He fixes himself a glass of cranberry juice, takes a sip of it, and cleans my face.

"Take your time son and tell me what happened. I know you weren't in a fight tonight. I'm sure it wasn't that. The tone of your voice expresses something more intense than a fight," Dad notices.

Words can't fully express what happened tonight. I wouldn't be able to capture the evil sentiment that happened, so I pull out my phone and go to my video gallery. I pull up the video of the incident that Kelsey sent me. I might as well let my dad watch the entire thing. They say a picture is worth a thousand words, so I know this video is worth a million words. I slide the phone over to my dad.

"Just hit the play button Dad. You'll see what happened for yourself," I verbalize.

Dad watches the video from start to finish. He's visibly frustrated by what he's watching. He rubs his chin and then rubs his head. My dad gets up and stands before me.

"Son, you handled the situation as best as you could have. You did nothing wrong tonight. The cops were totally wrong and it won't go unnoticed or unpunished. I'm sorry about what happened to Josh. I know he was your friend," Dad voices.

"Thanks Dad. As the cops assaulted us, all I could picture was you and your teachings. I really felt like you were out there with me. It's crazy, but you comforted me while I was out there on the ground," I narrate.

"I've never wanted you to have to experience police brutality or any other violence for that matter, but I'm glad you made it home safely. It comforts me to know that you were comforted by me during a chaotic time in your life. That's why I talk to you so much about life and I repeat myself a lot, but it's for a reason. It's to instill these things in your mind, so you'll have my teachings with you when I'm not," Dad explains.

"It all makes sense Dad. I get it now. I'll be honest with you, I used to think your lectures were overkill and redundant, but I don't anymore. When we were on the side of the highway, I kinda felt like I had the answers to a test. I knew what to expect," I state.

"That's good son. Everything I do and say is intentional. I don't make haphazard moves or comments. You should know that by now. You have to pay attention to me," Dad lectures.

"I know Dad. You're the man. Hands down…. You're the man and I can't deny that," I reply.

"You better listen because I'll be old soon and won't be able to take care of myself one day. You know I'm banking on you to be my backup plan," Dad jokes.

"Dad, you're in great shape. You'll be fine, but I got you though. Trust me, I got your back like how you have mine," I respond.

My dad and I talk about how I feel about the incident and then the conversation branches to a million other things. We talk for hours about the past and the future. Dad has the perfect blend of comfort and support without being mushy. My father is very manly, but not harsh and is very considerate. I respect him to the highest degree. My father asks me one more time if I'm okay. I tell him that I'm fine now and he retires for the night.

The next morning my dad wakes me up for breakfast. While we eat breakfast, he informs me that he has to take an emergency business trip to meet with some business constituents. He hates that he has to leave on the heels of the police occurrence, but assures me that it's completely necessary that he takes the trip. We finish eating and I go back upstairs to shower. Moments later, my father yells into the bathroom that he's going to leave.

I finish showering and getting dressed then I go downstairs to hit school. When I walk outside, I see my dad's car still in the garage. I didn't expect him to still be here. I thought he left already. I shoot back inside to see if he's still home, but there's no trace of him. He must have caught an Uber or one of his colleagues came to pick him up. Shucks, I hope Dr. Robinson came to pick him up. I'm running late to school now, so I hurry out the door and head to my future alma mater.

When I get to school, everyone's broken up about Josh being murdered. The entire student body is revved up and not focused. None of us are going to class because it just doesn't seem right that Josh's not here with us. The district has hired grief counselors to help us deal with the situation, but nobody's taking advantage of their help. We all just hang in the hallways with one another. We want to riot at the school to show our support for Josh, but that would be senseless because Linden didn't do anything to us. We'd only be hurting ourselves if we tore our school up. Jay walks up and gives me a pound.

"I can't believe they killed Josh. He was a brother to me. These pigs just took his life from him like he was a piece of shitty toilet paper that they were discarding. This is not the end of this situation," I remark.

Jay asks, "You know he was a brother to me too? How is this not the end of it? What are you planning to do?"

"Well, you know they're holding a candlelight vigil for him tonight at the courthouse in Bridgewater, so we'll go to that and protest this injustice," I reply.

Jay states, "Yeah, that's a good idea. We'll let them know that we're not standing for those cops just getting away with murder."

"Right, and what's even worse is that you know if it were some black cops who killed a white kid, they would be crucified immediately. They'll see us protesting peacefully and they'll have to do the right thing," I remark.

Jay replies, "Nayr, I don't know about that. You're thinking pretty optimistically and that's cool, but you know how they do us. Those cops will probably get off with no charges."

"No, not this time. We have the situation in its entirety on video. There's no way they walk this time. This one's a slam dunk. You saw the video of what happened. They can't walk," I comment.

"Bruh, we've seen this happen too many times to think that they'll be charged. You know that they protect their own. They'll probably flip it to make it seem like the killing was justified. I hope not, but I don't trust the police like that. Hell no," Jay replies.

"I feel you. I hope not though. Man, I just want this day to be over now. I can't even focus on anything other than what happened to Josh. I keep replaying the events of the night over and over again in my head," I state.

"I couldn't imagine watching one of my boys getting murdered in front of me. That video was tough enough to watch, so I know being there in person was brutal. Almost like torture," Jay voices.

"All I can say is unbelievable. I was hoping when I woke up this morning that it would all be a bad dream, but unfortunately it wasn't. I guess I couldn't be so lucky. Josh's family is devastated," I utter.

I punch my locker located in the second floor tunnel and then slam it shut. Next, I kick it so hard that I leave a dent in the door. I hate having this feeling of helplessness. I mean there's literally nothing we can do to help the situation. I can't finish this school day because I may hurt someone. Jay attempts to calm me down, but his efforts are futile.

"I'm outta here!" I yell.

"Word? Where are you headed?" Jay asks.

"I'm headed to the Marks. Maybe shoot around for a while. Basketball has always been a place of refuge for me," I answer.

Jay words, "Cool, I'm going with you. I don't feel like being here either. Can't concentrate myself. Shooting around doesn't sound bad."

Jay and I walk out of the tunnel and head for the stairway leading out of the building. As we are walking out the building, we see the more of our friends and they want to know where we're going. I tell them that we are headed to the Marks to play ball and they decide to roll with us. We all ditch school and go to the park to shoot around and take our minds off of this unfortunate incident. While we're at the park, more cars keep pulling up with students from the high school.

Jay posted pictures to Snapchat with us at the park, so many students ditched school to hit the park too. Even girls are pulling up to the park to chill with us. The park now looks like it's a high school basketball game with Linden playing a rivalry game against Elizabeth. I'm sure the school administrators will hear about this impromptu cut party, but who cares. An in-school suspension for cutting class is worth it in my book.

We play several games of basketball and it takes my mind off of things. This is one amazing block party we are having. We even have music playing while we play ball and chill. Several hours pass and the crowd diminishes. It's time to head to the vigil being held in Bridgewater, so I drive home to take a shower and head out. Jay goes home to get cleaned up and is meeting me at my house, so we can ride together.

An hour later, I hear my doorbell ring and it's Jay. He's ready to head over to Bridgewater and so am I. We jump in Jay's car and before long, we arrive at the courthouse. There's an immense crowd already formed. Everyone's peaceful and singing songs of peace. Jay and I fall right in line with everyone else and begin singing too. We are really protestors. I never imagined that I would be in this situation, but I am and it feels good. I'm proud to be here.

After about an hour of gathering peacefully, we notice more and more police presence. They actually have us surrounded. The police are in full riot gear and are on their bullhorns telling us that we have to disperse. We know our rights and know that we have a right to protest, so nobody moves. In fact, many people sit down on the ground in an effort to show the police that we aren't going anywhere. The police issue an ultimatum to us.

Nobody adheres to their ultimatum, so the police officers begin to pepper spray the crowd. Many people begin coughing and choking from being sprayed. Next, the cops start pushing people with their riot shields and even hit some gatherers with their night sticks. Some are even thrown to the ground and beaten while in handcuffs. When Jay and I regain our composure from being sprayed, we make a beeline to the car.

"Fuck this shit! We tried to show our disapproval the peaceful way, but that didn't work. Fuck it, we just have to fight fire with fire!" I scream as I sit in the passenger seat of Jay's car.

"Hell yeah! We have no other choice!" Jay speaks.

"Those white bastards killed one of our boys, and when we protest peacefully they resort to violence against us. Well, I'm not taking this sitting down anymore. By any means necessary," I orate.

"You know I ride with you? What you wanna do?" Jay inquires.

I tell Jay the plan and we go riding. While we're riding, we see who we're looking for. We see an unsuspecting white boy who looks like an easy target jogging down the street. We drive past him and park up ahead. We know he'll be jogging up to us at any minute, so we squat and wait. Two minutes later he is on us. I take a stick that I found on the ground and crack him over the head with it. He falls to the ground immediately. I hit him so hard that the stick breaks into two pieces. Jay goes to stomp him out, but I stop him.

"Don't stomp him. The last thing we need is any evidence connecting us to him. If you use your feet, there may be blood transferred to your clothes and then we'll be busted," I say.

"Okay, I got you. Well, I'll just hit him with the other half of the stick you used," Jay replies.

He grabs the stick and we both pummel him repeatedly. The attack lasts about thirty more seconds and then we break camp. We can't be seen over here. The good thing is that there are many people in this area who are only around for the protest, so it'll be hard for the police to pinpoint who did this to him. Jay and I make it back to my house with no problems. Jay cracks jokes about how he was like Barry Bonds when he hit the white guy with the stick.

"That small payback feels real damn good!" I announce.

"Yeah, I agree. Bruh, he fell hard as hell when you initially hit him. That was epically hilarious. Definitely one for the books," Jay speaks.

"It's sad that we had to resort to that, but we were forced to retaliate. I've never been a violent person, but when my back is against the wall, I will always do what I have to do," I explain.

"I see that. He's probably on the news by now. I'm about to turn on the television to see what's going on with our attack," Jay mouths.

He turns on the television and surfs the channels, but we don't see anything. The only coverage is from the rally in Bridgewater. It shows us being pepper sprayed and beat down like animals. They love to show things that depict African Americans being harmed or ridiculed.

"I hope they broadcast that white boy we beat down. White America needs to see this happening more often, so they'll understand how we feel when our brothers are beaten or killed. It's a shame that people need to feel great suffering to understand how someone else feels when they suffer a great loss," I say.

"It's crazy that it's like that, but that's the way the world works. Nobody knows how much it hurts to lose a loved one, until they lose a loved one themselves," Jay verbalizes.

"I bet if those cops knew that one of their family members would be killed if they murdered a black person for nothing, they wouldn't be so quick to shoot. They would be much more prudent in their decision making when it comes to taking a black life," I vocalize.

"Of course, they'd think twice about it if they knew Sally or Amy would be murdered. I bet black people wouldn't be harmed ever again. The thing is they know that there are no consequences for their actions, so they proceed recklessly," Jay states.

"Well, we did our part tonight. I wish there was a way to alert the media of what we did without getting caught. We could start a movement of anytime a black life is lost unjustly, that we retaliate by taking a white life," I say. "That'll cease all of the unarmed black killings."

Jay and I talk some more and then he leaves. I throw my clothes in the wash, jump in the shower and head to bed.

CHAPTER 6
Harry's Perspective

I'm finally back from my conference. I have to admit that I never expected to be gone for longer than a week's time, but things didn't go as smoothly as I anticipated. My travel plans were not as specific as I had hoped. The good thing is that I did make it to my intended destination and met with the people I wanted to. The meeting was a success overall. Unfortunately, we did lose valuable time for the conference stemming from our travel plans being messed up, so some language historians decided to come here to New Jersey to finish up what we needed to do. I'm glad to return home and see that my boy still has the house intact. He didn't even leave any dishes in the sink. I grab a bottle of water out of the refrigerator and have a seat. Moments later, Nayr comes downstairs to the kitchen.

"Dad, I didn't hear you come in. I would have been downstairs had I known you were back," asserts Nayr.

"Yes, I'm back. I popped into the house to see if I could catch you doing something you weren't supposed to be doing. I guess you're clean because everything looks good around here," I utter.

"Dad, you know I behave myself, don't you? How was the business trip? Is your phone broken or something?" Nayr asks.

I reply, "I know you behave yourself, but you are a teenage boy. I was your age at one point a long time ago. Thanks for asking and the trip was very productive. I'm glad I went when I did. In fact, some of my colleagues traveled back to Linden with me, so we could finish up. I don't want you to be surprised if you see them floating around here even though they aren't staying here. I have them staying in a hotel on 1&9. Actually, I accidentally left my phone downstairs in my lab. It was a total bonehead move because I was lost without it."

"Okay, I was only asking because I texted you a couple of times, but you didn't respond. I figured you were fine. I didn't think about checking your lab for your phone," Nayr comments.

"How are things with you? How are you holding up?" I ask.

"Dad, everything's good. I'm holding up just fine. I'm even better now that you're back. Not too much is going on here. I'm just ready for this school year to be over. I have a major case of 'senioritis' on my chest, but I'll get through. I've inherited my father's mental fortitude," Nayr remarks.

"Fantastic. I want you to know that I'll be looking into the incident with Josh and the police that occurred before I left. I'll definitely get some of my lawyer friends to investigate that entire fiasco. Justice will prevail one way or the other," I assure.

"I know Dad. You never take an injustice lightly. I'll testify or do whatever I have to do to help out. We could end up with a healthy lawsuit from this Pop. We'll be rich from this!" Nayr speaks.

"There are things bigger and more important than money. As long as justice is served, I will be perfectly fine with that. I just like for things to be equal. Unfortunately, when it comes to that, we'll be going up against a judicial system that's not for us. If you're not for us, you're against us," I narrate.

"Right, but I'm still hoping for some money from this. We deserve it. I could go for the life of a millionaire," my son says.

I communicate, "I could go for a few extra million myself, but I'm not banking on it. I'll just keep going to work and stacking these millions little by little."

"That's a definite Dad. I'm headed to school," Nayr claims.

"Have a good day son. Make sure you learn something. Oh yeah, I may have your sweetheart Dr. Robinson over. Before you get too excited, just know the visit is work related," I assert.

"That's straight Dad, but just know that my last three girlfriends started out being tutored by me and then the relationships got real personal," Nayr blurts as he runs out the door grinning. "I'm sure yours and Dr. Robinson's relationship won't be any different."

Nayr goes to school and I call Dr. Robinson. She too has called and texted me while I was away, so I know she'll be happy to hear from me. I know I can't wait to hear her sweet voice again. I hated not having my phone while I was gone. I felt like I was on a deserted island. These cell phones are addictive.

"Hello, may I speak to Dr. Robinson?" I ask.

"This is she. I started to think I offended you because you hadn't returned my calls or texts over the last several days," Dr. Robinson conveys.

I quickly dispel her thoughts, "I'm sorry you thought that, but that wasn't the case. Not one bit. I was negligent and forgot my phone at home while I was on a business trip. As sweet as you are, you could never make me not want to talk to you."

"That's very sweet of you. Also, that's good to know. I know not having your phone had to suck. I've forgotten my phone at home while on a trip and I almost cried daily. I felt so isolated. Well, I hope the rest of your trip was fruitful," Dr. Robinson states.

I respond, "Yes, it was great besides missing you."

"Are you flirting with me?" she asks.

"It all depends on if you are flattered or not," I retort.

"I have a big smile on my face, so I guess I'm flattered. Thank you, for making me smile," she replies.

I say, "Anytime. I almost forgot why I called. I wanted to know if you have any free time in your schedule to come to Linden. It will be for very pressing business and maybe we can mix a little personal time in with it. I'll pay for your travel and lodging, of course."

"I know my schedule is very tight after tomorrow. I'll be on the west coast for better than a month. If it's not tomorrow, it will be clear into next month," she communicates.

"Listen, it's still early. I'll call the airline now and book your flight for today. Then we'll have the rest of the day to meet and most of tomorrow. You can fly back home tomorrow afternoon," I explain.

"This must be very important, so I'll make it for sure. There's no need to book a flight because I'm currently in Maryland, so I'll just drive up. Send me your address and I'll see you in a few hours," she verbalizes.

"Doctor, it's not important... No, it's urgent! I'm glad you are free. It's fortuitous that you're so close too. I'll send my address as soon as we hang up," I speak.

I send her my address and she sends back a message stating that she received the text. It's only a three hour drive from Maryland to New Jersey, so I need to get a move on it. The house is pretty clean, but I still feel the need to tighten it up a little more. I don't want Dr. Robinson to see something that I overlooked and think I keep a dirty house. Honestly, aside from work, I hope to impress her and make her want to come back to visit me personally. I don't know if she'll be willing to stay in my guest room or not, but I'll prepare it just in case she's okay with it.

I also go online to check some rates at the hotel that I have my colleagues from the conference staying at. I'll be ready to present Dr. Robinson with this info when she arrives. Lastly, I go upstairs and shave and shower. I was unable to shave while I was away, so my facial hair is out of control. I get dressed after the shower and run to the liquor store to purchase some wine.

I return home and put the wine on ice. Shortly after two o'clock, I hear a car pulling into my driveway. I look out of the window and see a black seven series BMW sitting there. I'm not expecting anyone other than Dr. Robinson, so I assume that it's her. Seconds later, my phone rings. It's the doctor telling me that she's outside.

I go outside to greet her. I walk over to her car door and open it. She gets out and gives me a very warm embrace. I'm totally caught off guard by this pleasant surprise, but I don't act like it. Her perfume invades my nostrils and slightly turns me on.

"How was your drive?" I ask.

"The drive was fine. I didn't meet any traffic, so my travels were pretty uninterrupted," she answers.

"That's good. And thanks again for coming up on such short notice. Come on, let's talk inside," I voice. "You coming really means a lot."

"Don't mention it, but you better make it worth my while," she says with a smile.

I don't know if she's talking slick or not, so I don't comment the way I really want to. I'll give her the benefit of the doubt that her comment was innocent. If it wasn't innocent, I'll find out later in the visit. We walk inside and I show her around my home.

Dr. Robinson states, "You have a beautiful home. It's also so very clean! I'm impressed."

"Thank you. I try to live orderly. I've never been one to live in clutter," I announce.

"That's astonishing because many bachelors live in a pigsty. I'm glad to see that you aren't one of them. A lady could get comfortable in here," she comments.

I remark, "You should get comfy then. I have no problem with that."

"Is that right?" she asks.

"Absolutely. Where are my manners? Would you like something to drink or eat?" I ask.

"Yes, a glass of wine if you have some," she informs.

I fix her a glass of wine and then we head downstairs to my lab. Dr. Robinson is more impressed by my lab than she was by the rest of the house. My lab has my life's work inside of it, so it pleases me that she appreciates it. That lets me know that I'm doing something right down here.

"So, what kind of work do you do down here?" she inquires.

I describe some of the projects I'm currently working on in my lab. Some of the things I detail she fully comprehends, while other things are a little gray. I do my best to get her up to speed on what I do. I'm stunned that she understands as much as she does. Most people outside the field of physics only understand a very small percentage of what I explain.

"I'll be honest, it seems like you have a handle on things. I don't see how or why you need my help," she admits.

"I've studied your model and notes on plate tectonics and it makes sense, but I'm still missing something. Let me show you a calculation I did based on what you presented at Georgetown University," I reply.

I show her my formula for calculating how far Africa has drifted away from The United States of America over the last 450 years. She looks at my figures and sees my error immediately.

"I see you have the landmass drift annually at .6 inches per year and that's precise, but you don't accommodate for erosion of the continents. That figure has to be accounted for in your math. If it's not accounted for, your distance could be off by miles depending on how much erosion took place as well as how much of a time span you are looking at," Dr. Robinson explains.

"That makes perfect sense. Thanks for clarifying this for me," I verbalize.

"No problem. It's like going into outer space to find Mars and being a thousandth of a mile off in your calculation. Just imagine how far from Mars you would be by the time you entered into outer space," she speaks.

"You're likely to never find it. You'd be more likely to find another planet," I say comically.

"Exactly! I know you didn't have me drive here for a fictional mathematical equation. I still don't see how this ties into your work," she says.

"I love information. Your presentation intrigued me. That's all," I reply.

"Harry, I have two doctoral degrees. However, I'm not only book smart, I have an enormous amount common sense too. I know this equation isn't for nothing. Fill me in," she verbalizes.

I have no choice, but to bring her up to speed on what's going on and what I need the calculation for. I tell her how this information will help me going forward. She is flabbergasted by what I disclose to her. She even questions if I'm telling jokes or if I'm really telling the truth. I assure her that I don't joke when it comes to my research.

She takes my word for it and promises not to share this information with anyone. The last thing I need is for the word to get out about my research prematurely. The government would raid my lab and lock me away forever or just kill me right away before I can talk to anyone. I inform her of how it works. We stay in the lab for hours conversing.

By the time we come upstairs, it's dark outside. I completely forgot to ask her about sleeping here or at the hotel. She decides to stay here at the house because of the lateness of the hour. That's good for me because I feel a penny saved is a penny earned. I go to the car and grab her luggage. When I come back in, I direct her to follow me to the guest bedroom.

I drop her belongings off in the room. We say our goodnights to each other and part ways. Moments later, I hear the shower running. I know it's not Nayr because he hasn't gotten home yet. I decide to study some more before I go to sleep.

While I'm studying, I hear the shower stop running and hear the doctor getting in the bed. Twenty minutes later I turn off my reading light in an attempt to get some sleep. Suddenly, I hear a knock at my door. The last time I had a knock at my door, it was my son telling me he was assaulted by the cops. I hope that's not the case again.

"It's open. Come in," I voice.

To my delight, it's Dr. Robinson and she's dressed in a simple silk women's pajama suit. Apparently, she couldn't get comfortable in the guest bed. She claims that it's too lumpy and will kill her back. I apologize to her for the inconvenience and tell her she can have my bed and I'll sleep in the guest bedroom.

"There's no need for you to mess your back up. I'll just sleep in here with you. I'm sure your bed isn't lumpy like that one is," she speaks.

"It's definitely a memory foam mattress and it's very comfortable," I assure.

Dr. Robinson gets in the bed with me before I can even tell her it's okay. She surprises me by not getting at the foot of the bed. We are resting face to face and talking in the dark. This night is going better than I expected. I text my son that Dr. Robinson is here and he asks if he can stay at Jay's place.

I tell him that it's not a problem. He informs me that he'll be home in the morning to change clothes for school. Dr. Robinson smells like she is fresh out of Bath and Body Works. I want to touch her, but I don't want to offend her. I haven't had a woman in this room since my wife was alive. It feels good and weird at the same time.

The more we lie in bed and talk, the closer our bodies get. Now my leg is on her and I'm sensually caressing her leg with mine. She responds by putting one of her arms on me. Not too long later, we are cuddling. She has her head on my chest and I have my arm around her cradling her closely.

The next thing I know, it's morning. I'm awakened by Nayr fumbling around in the kitchen. Dr. Robinson is still asleep on my chest. We fell asleep while engulfed in deep conversation. Last night was very special. I appreciated every minute of it. I tap Dr. Robinson to wake her up, but she doesn't budge. I ease her off of my chest, so I don't wake her up. I get out the bed and go downstairs to talk to Nayr.

When I get downstairs, Nayr looks at me with a boyish grin. It's like he's proud of me or something. I know he thinks I had sex last night, but I didn't. Last night was bigger than sex; it was an investment into the future. Last night we made love to each other's minds. What happened last night was sapiosexual and was far more pleasurable than sexual intercourse. Falling in love with a woman's mind lasts a lifetime. I talk to my son before he leaves for school and then I prepare breakfast for my guest.

I finish cooking breakfast, put it on a plate, and take it upstairs. Dr. Robinson is just waking up as I open the door.

"Something smells delicious," she states.

"Yes, it's breakfast in bed for my guest," I say.

"It not only smells delicious, it looks delicious too. Thank you so much," she speaks.

"You're welcome," I utter.

She eats her breakfast while I freshen up. When I get out of the shower, I take her plate to the kitchen and clean up. She heads to the shower and gets dressed. She eventually meets me downstairs in the kitchen. We head down to the lab for a few hours to work before Dr. Robinson departs. Just before she leaves, she gives me a juicy kiss on the lips. This is definitely a successful encounter. I'm on cloud nine.

CHAPTER 7
Harry's Perspective

It's been two weeks since Dr. Robinson came to visit. Her help with my research was invaluable. She was able to clear up some vital mistakes I was making in my mathematical equations. I am forever indebted to her. I hope she gets done with her work out on the west coast early, so maybe she can come back to visit me. We've talked or texted every day since she left my home.

I'm happy that my career is flourishing. I've made great advances in my research and my students at the university are flourishing academically. Additionally, my personal life is prospering. My son has a full scholarship to college and we have a fantastic father-son relationship. I can proudly admit that our bond is one that is unbreakable. Lastly, my love life has taken a turn for the better. I'm excited about the possibility of a relationship with Dr. Robinson.

It was fortunate that Kelsey and Ashley recorded the police unlawfully stopping and assaulting my son the night they murdered Josh. They posted the video to Facebook and it went viral basically overnight. Millions of people viewed the video and there was an overwhelming amount of public outrage. I also made a couple of phone calls to some politically connected people. They were able to put some pressure on the prosecutors to sway them to bring charges on the cops involved with my son's incident.

Fortunately, the cops were arrested and charged with first degree murder. Only one of them has been bailed out. I guess that million dollar bail isn't so easy to come by. Those cops being arrested and charged is a step in the right direction, but it doesn't mean that justice is served. The only thing that's acceptable is a conviction for the murder. If the cops get off, it will be a total disappointment and a failure of the judicial system.

I hear my phone ringing from upstairs. I whisk to my room to get it. I see Nayr's face on my phone's screen as I reach to grab it. I answer the phone call.

"Hello, son," I say.

Nayr starts talking a mile a minute as soon as he hears my voice. He's talking so loud and fast that his words are unintelligible. It sounds like he's running too. There's a tremendous amount of background noise. I'm starting to think that maybe Nayr called me accidentally.

"Son, can you hear me? Are you there?" I ask urgently.

He answers in a faint whisper, "Yes, I can hear you. I'm being chased."

In a concerned voice I inquire, "Chased?! Chased for what and by whom? Where are you son?"

"I was on Route 22 in Mountainside at the movies. When I came out the theater, my car had been spray-painted with the word nigger on the driver's side door. I was unaffected by it because I remember what you told me. It's just words on a car, so I proceeded to come home. While I was driving through town, some white kids were beside me screaming and hollering racial epithets and one dude was screaming that I had his dad arrested. Next thing I know, they had me blocked in somewhere on Michigan Avenue, so I jumped out the car and ran," I report.

"You have to be kidding me. I'm coming to get you. Where are you now?" I ask.

"Wait, I hear them coming," Nayr says whispering.

I jump up and sprint to the car. The line is quiet and I understand why. Nayr doesn't want to alert whoever's after him to his whereabouts. I get in the car and head in the direction of where my son is. I want to call the cops to tell them what's going on, but I don't know if the cops in that area will be willing to assist the person who many people feel is responsible for their comrades being incarcerated.

"Dad, are you still there?" Nayr murmurs.

"Yes, I'm still here. I'm on my way to get you," I voice.

"Dad, all I know is that I'm on top of a shed. It's really like a barn. They chased me and I was able to get ahead of them, so they lost sight of me. I dipped into this barn, climbed a ladder, and now I'm hiding. They're on the first level looking for me. I can hear them," Nayr explains.

"Just sit tight," I order.

"Somebody's climbing the ladder," Nayr remarks.

I respond, "Son, you've trained for this for years. Use the skills I taught you while hunting and competing in those paintball competitions. It's all the same. Don't respond. I know you can hear me."

Nayr doesn't say anything else, but I can hear someone yelling vulgar terms as they look for him. I need to get there now. I've probably aged ten years in the last 15 minutes while heading to rescue my son. I get to the block that he's on. I see a huge shed in the backyard of this house. I still have my ear to the phone when I hear someone say that they've found the nigger. I have to play this just right because I don't want an incident with these people. I run to the shed and quietly slide the door open just enough to see in.

Someone screams, "Get your snitch ass up, nigger!"

Another person states, "Snitches get stitches you black bitch! And your stiches are coming right now!"

As Nayr is about to get assaulted for sure, I yell out, "This is the police. You are trespassing and need to leave the premises now. You will be arrested if we find you in here. We are coming in this shed in ten seconds!"

Fortunately, I hear a bunch of people saying that they are out of here. I peek inside and see several boys jumping out of the side windows of the barn. Everyone scatters to my delight.

"Son, are you clear?" I ask as I speak into the phone.

"Well, I'm clear of the people who were after me, but the police are outside now. I still can't leave this barn," Nayr speaks. "I'm still screwed."

"That was me faking as the police son. Come from your hiding spot. We have to get out of here before the police really do show up," I order.

He climbs down the ladder and we head for the car. My son is rattled and relieved all at the same time. I tell him that he's safe now and doesn't need to be shaken anymore. I drive him back to his car, so he can take it home. I follow him all the way back to Linden. He calls me while I'm following him.

"Son, is everything alright?" I ask.

"Everything's all good, but I have a question for you," Nayr voices.

I respond, "Ask anything."

"How were you able to find me even when I didn't know exactly where I was?" Nayr questions.

"That was simple. I tracked your iPhone through the find my iPhone feature. I pulled you up and drove right to you. I'm glad you listened to your pop and left the feature activated. I would hate to think what would have happened to you otherwise," I explain.

"I totally forgot about that feature. I never would have thought to use it. I'm glad you did Dad. Those guys had me cornered," Nayr remarks. "I was in a very precarious situation."

"A situation can never get too bad as long as you keep your cool and never stop thinking. Fear and panic disable rational thought. One lacking rational thought is rendered useless," I explain.

We arrive home safe and sound. It's sad that my son has to be victimized after he was the victim. He's not the reason why those cops were arrested, so it's hurtful to me that he has to pay the price for those cops' wrongdoings. I can't have my son being threatened every time he leaves the house. I have to correct this now.

I drive to the hotel where my colleagues have been staying. I bring them back to the house because they'll be leaving in the morning. We arrive back at the house and I make them pallets to sleep on. They don't mind their sleeping arrangements. They're like me in that they've slept on a pallet or two in their day. The hotel is fairly close, but it's best that we're all gathered here before they depart. Nayr helps me with their pallets. While we're making the pallets, I inform him that I too will be leaving tomorrow. He takes the news well even though he wants me to stick around.

"Dad, do you have to go with them?" Nayr inquires.

"Son, you know I do. I'll only be gone a few days, but I do have to go. I wouldn't leave if someone else could take my place," I convey.

Nayr and I talk for a while longer before I go to my room. Nayr follows me to my room, so we can continue talking. I eventually fall asleep on him.

Morning is here and I wake my son and house guests up. We eat breakfast and then we prepare to leave.

"Dad, do you need help with your bags? Where are they, so I can throw them in the car?" Nayr asks.

"Thanks son, but we're fine with the bags. We'll manage. You should head to school now," I say.

"Enjoy your trip Dad and make sure you follow the rule while you're gone," my son utters.

"What's that son?" I inquire.

"Be safe!" Nayr answers.

"Oh, that's first and foremost. I'll be safe and you make sure you are too," I vocalize.

My son walks out the door for school and my colleagues and I leave for our trip.

CHAPTER 8
Harry's Perspective

Fortunately, we arrive in Africa in no time. My travel situation is a lot better than it was last time. I have to thank Dr. Robinson for that. With her assistance, this time around is perfect. Everyone has their luggage, so there were no hiccups in that regard either. We're only a mile or two from where we will be conducting our business.

Craig and Phil are two colleagues of mine from the United States who are accompanying me during this trip. We will be staying off the coast of the Senegal River. Our other colleagues who are attending the conference are staying further inland. They'll join us tomorrow with their other constituents for all day gatherings. We'll be meeting and strategizing for the rest of the week. I know one thing and that is it's burning up out here. I already miss the amenities from back home for the time being, but I signed up for it, so I have to make the best of the situation. The work we're doing here will be well worth it. Sometimes you have to sacrifice to get what you want out of life. You may have to take two steps backwards to take three steps forward.

My colleagues and I enjoy the beautiful coastline for the rest of the day. We don't venture too far out because we are unfamiliar with the area, but the beach is close enough for us to venture to. What an amazingly wonderful continent. I can't wait to explore the rest of it. Unfortunately, I can't explore the continent now because this is a business trip. The beach is pristine without a piece of trash in sight. The sand is the purest white I've ever seen in my life. It's so well preserved that from a distance it looks like freshly fallen snow. Wow, this is the home of my ancestors. Nayr has to come here one day.

I didn't sleep nearly as poorly as I thought I would. Surprisingly, I feel at peace here this time. I guess the last time wasn't as enjoyable because it was my first time coming and I didn't know what to expect from this foreign land. Not to mention, our travels were a bit off and caused me a great deal of inconvenience. I have no idea what time it is. I can only refer to the time of day as sunrise and a beautiful sunrise it is. What feels like a few hours after sunrise, all of the attendees of the meeting arrive.

All of the leaders of the groups have talked to

their people and have them up to speed on what is to take place today if our guests arrive on schedule. From what I understand, the weather has been fine, so they should be on time. We wait for hours in the heat, but no one shows up. We wasted a full day doing nothing when we could have been productive. We see no visitors during the day and none show up at night, so we call it quits.

Fortunately, no one leaves because it wouldn't make sense. The visitors could show up at any minute, so it's best that everyone stays put. As we camp out in the woods, we are awakened by the noise of sailboats approaching the coastline. They seem to be anchoring where they are off shore right now. I know they can't see us because I can barely see my hand in front of my face. It's dark like a bottomless pit. The only reason I can think of them anchoring at such a far distance is to ensure they don't crash up against any rocks. This is the slave coast, so we knew it was only a matter of time before our guests showed up.

Hours later when the sun has risen, they raise their anchors and begin to make their way closer to shore. I feel the hair on the back of my neck standing up. I've never felt a rush like this before in my life. For years white people have argued that they weren't the ones who enslaved blacks and they're right. They weren't directly responsible for it, but their ancestors were and white people have been reaping the benefits of the slave trade ever since.

To the contrary, my ancestors were slaves and black people have been suffering ever since. We built a nation that doesn't treat us fairly and doesn't respect us as people. I wish more tribal leaders refused to sell Africans as slaves like Jaja of Opobo of Nigeria. With more rulers like him around, maybe slavery could have been stopped before it started.

We send some men to wave the ships in closer and to provide assurance that everything's normal. We even have some men staged as slaves on a platform where they would normally be sold from. Now, it's time I meet the actual slave traders face to face. I have all sorts of anger built up inside of me. I hope I can control myself when I look pure evil and hatred in the eye. My years of planning are finally about to pay off.

"Here those blue-eyed devils come. This is the moment I've been waiting for! On my cue I want you to open fire, but not a second before. We have to make sure they are all in our line of fire. We can't have any of them turn around and escape," I dictate.

"When do you want us to stop firing on them? Should we wait for your cue to cease firing too?" asks Craig.

"No, don't wait for my cue. You don't stop shooting until there's no movement coming from them. You don't stop until they're all sent to hell.

That's the only sign you'll need," I reply sternly.

We lie and wait for a few more minutes and allow them to get a little closer. Once they're closer, they'll be to the point of no return. This is a major step in attaining victory. It is crucial that we are victorious today.

"Get ready men! Get ready! Today's battle is not just for us, it's for our parents, our parents' parents, and our kids' kids. Almost there... Almost there... They're not going to know what hit them. Ready... Aim... Fire... Give them hell!" I order.

Gun fire erupts, decimating the silence and calm of the day. Gunshots bang through the air like fireworks over the Hudson River during Fourth of July celebrations. The fifty calibers we brought will take down these old wooden ships in no time. The smiles the white devils have on their faces suddenly turn to looks of horror. I bet those conniving bastards shit in their pants too. They thought today was going be sweet for them, but it's not. However, it's going to be sweet for us.

As expected, the white men aboard the slave ships don't take our attack lightly. They grab their weapons and take a defensive stance to fight back. Our weapons are far more superior than theirs. We have hundreds of years' worth of technological advances to our weaponry. Their weapons are primitive. Our weapons are more accurate and can fire more rapidly than theirs.

We also have centuries of proven battle tactics to use to our advantage. This battle is really over before it started.

The men on board the ships fire their primitive weapons that don't come close to where we are firing from with the .50 caliber rifles we have. The ships are taking heavy fire and are being torn to shreds. The white men have five men teams assembled to help fire the cannons they have on the ship. The firing distance of the cannons is further than we calculated. The explosions from the cannons are very close to us. We can't lose this battle and we can't be pushed back.

Sadly, we begin to take many casualties. The reason we're taking casualties is because their weapons are better than we anticipated and many of our fighters are giving up their cover and running into the open while firing at the ships. The cannons are blowing our men's limbs off and killing them. We hear the screams of our brothers in battle and we can see and hear that they are in agonizing pain. I know they are warriors, but they were told to never give up their positions.

"Take out the cannons," I order. "We have to take out the cannons now!"

Some of us focus our attention on destroying the cannons or at least taking out the men who are manning them. With our attention concentrated on the cannons, we take them down. The .50 calibers continue ripping holes into the bodies of the white men. One of our fighters manages to make his way into the water and is able to throw a grenade onto the closest vessel. The grenade explodes and kills several men on board. That ship begins to sink. As the cannon balls explode on the beach, sand plumes forty feet in the air. Smoke infiltrates the air and resembles an early foggy morning. The smell of gunpowder permeates the air to the point where you can choke on it. As our men are riddled with gunfire, the shoreline becomes stained with crimson blood. We embrace our journey for freedom head on.

Once the first ship begins to sink, the men on the other ship throw down their weapons and raise white flags. They know they will meet the exact same fate if they continue to fight. We order the slave traders to jump into the water and swim to shore. As they swim to shore, we deploy paddle boats to round them up. It's a small victory, but a victory it is.

Unfortunately, another enemy ship manned by the white devils comes into our line of sight. They begin to fire on us with their cannons and rifles. They're going to go down. I take cover again behind a platform that was designed to load slaves onto slave ships. I fire rapidly at the ship and hit it several times. I see several men on the ship torn to smithereens from my assault. They realize that they are outmatched in this fight because they turn the ship around and head back in the direction they came. The last thing we need is for one of the ships to get away. I jump up and run as close to the shoreline as I can get, while continuing to fire at the retreating ship. I throw down the .50 caliber and yank the RPG off of my back as I squat in the sand. I know I only have one shot at this, so I have to make it count. I prepare the RPG for fire and let her rip. Unfortunately, I do not hit the ship. The rocket flies through the air without hitting anything. I know I missed a valuable opportunity. Additionally, I know that the Portuguese will send more ships when they find out about this attack on them.

All of our men celebrate our victory today. The slave traders have been tied up and we interrogate them. They have very arrogant attitudes towards us. Even though they are our prisoners now, they still call us boys and niggers. They threaten us with taking our lives and ensuring that we'll be treated more severely than other slaves because of our actions. What makes them think that they will ever have that opportunity again? I've had enough of their idle threats, so I return back to my tent to get some rest. I'm leaving in the morning to go back home and get more supplies.

The next morning I wake up and my colleagues and I prepare to leave. I go to our vehicle, so we can depart and I see the most upsetting thing I've ever seen in my life. The vehicle has been damaged from the gun fight with the white men and we can't leave Africa. One of those cannons must have exploded close enough to damage it. I knew it was too close to the battle ground, but I didn't want to be too far from it because I feared it would be stolen. It appears that we are stuck.

"Smith, that looks very badly damaged. It doesn't look reparable. It's like a totaled car," Phil remarks.

"I'm sorry my friend, but there is no way I can fix this now. The items and technology needed to fix it just don't exist here at this time. There's no way around this. All we can do is wait, but don't worry, I have a backup plan," I respond.

"A backup plan?" Craig asks.

"Yes, I have a plan, but for now we need to rebuild and get strong again. We have to be ready for when another ship comes. History tells us that the British sent thousands of ships to Africa as well as thousands of slave trade voyages made by the Portuguese. They don't refer to this region as the Slave Coast for nothing," I explain.

"Well, I hope your backup plan consists of hundreds of men inundating this area because we are going to need them when the Portuguese return," Phil expresses with concern.

We call a meeting with the heads of the tribes to bring them up to speed on our current situation. They tell their men what's going on and that there will be more fighting in the next days, weeks, or months to come. If I'm lucky, I'll be out of here by then. For now, we are guests in the motherland. We're shown a king's hospitality.

CHAPTER 9
Nayr's Perspective

The school day is over and I'm home just chilling. Jay is coming over with some of our female friends from school. I'm looking forward to a few laughs tonight. No need to squander the weekend doing nothing, so a mini house party it is. We'll keep it high school age appropriate though. That means no drinking alcohol or smoking anything illegal, but I will indulge in some making out if the night goes in my favor. I'm a horny high school kid and I'm all for happy endings.

Around 6 p.m., Jay shows up to my crib. Our company will be over in about an hour. We have to get a game plan together for the night. The reason we need a plan is so that we don't shoot ourselves in the foot with the ladies who are coming over. The problem is that we're all just cool from school and we don't know which one of the females is interested in me and we don't know which one likes Jay. We know if either one of us makes a move on the wrong one, the night will be basically over.

Nobody likes to be the second choice. If one female finds out that the guy she likes wants her friend, that will spoil the mood and nobody will hook up with anybody. It can make for a very awkward situation and a tense night. Jay and I see eye to eye and get along very well, so it doesn't take too long to get our game plan set. After about thirty minutes of strategizing, Jay and I have it worked out. We decide not to make a move on any one of them and let the night flow naturally.

At 7:11, Jay receives a text from Kayla informing him that she and Christina are about to leave Christina's house to head to us. She tells Jay to text her my address. Neither one of them has ever been to my house before. Jay and I are stoked that they are coming through. By most students' accounts, Kayla and Christina are the two prettiest girls at the school and we have them coming over to chill with us.

The ride from Christina's house to mine is only about seven minutes long. However, it's 8 o'clock and they still haven't arrived. I know they say women always run late, but this is ridiculous. Jay and I are growing impatient, so Jay texts Kayla to see where they are. I mean blasting the music is fun, but it gets kind of boring when you're only looking at your best friend. Just after he sends the text, the girls ring the doorbell. I open the door and let them in.

"Sup? Took y'all long enough. We were about to ditch you two and call our second option for the night," I say jokingly.

Kayla speaks, "You could have done that, but whoever your second option is, is a second option for a reason. Just like we're the number one option for a reason. Don't trip."

They laugh and have a seat. They both have on the same outfit. They have on the low bred 11s, black leggings, and red crop tops with their stomachs exposed. They both smell like they bathed in Victoria's Secret's products. They both have their hair slicked back in ponytails with clear lens glasses on. I can honestly say that they are killing the game right now. Another thing I have to be honest about, but won't tell them, is that they are the first option and the only option for the night. They have our full attention.

"Nayr, I thought your dad wasn't here. I thought that was his Jag I saw in the garage. I know you and Jay aren't trying to chill with your dad chaperoning us," Christina comments.

"No, my dad isn't here. Jay told you that we have the house to ourselves and we do. My dad's away on business and left his car. You know we're not lame like that. Remember, Jay and me were your first options for a reason. You know me and Jay be lit!" I remark.

Kayla chimes in, "Yeah, whatever. You and Jay think you're lit, but we'll be the judge of that."

Jay voices, "Don't act like that because you know my party was the best party of the year if not, the best of our high school career. Me and Nayr had my party turnt!"

"Yeah, I can't front on that. Yo, your party was extra lit. The red carpet did it for me. I took a pic of the carpet and put it on Snapchat," Christina informs.

"Okay, so stop trying to roast. You know what it is," I verbalize.

The night with Kayla and Christina is going great! We're having a lot of fun talking, laughing, and playing cards. While we're playing cards, the D-lo Shuffle comes on Jay's playlist.

"Bruh, you have to do the D-lo Shuffle for me. I still don't know how to it," Christina says.

I question, "How don't you know how to do the D-lo? Don't you be acting like you're super lit?"

"They came in here roasting us, but they aren't so turnt themselves. Nayr, they aren't ready for us," Jay claims.

"We're definitely turnt, so stop it. Playing us like we're lame," Kayla shoots back.

Jay restarts the D-lo Shuffle from the beginning and we get into position. The song plays and we rock the dance from start to finish. Jay and I are in perfect synchronization. We don't miss a step throughout the entire song. The girls start feeling outdone, so they jump up and start twerking on us. Kayla dances with me and Christina dances with Jay. We're now engulfed in an all-out grind session. The song ends and then The Whip starts playing. Kayla and Christina stop dancing with us and they dance to The Whip. They have it down pact and don't miss a beat. They even have their own additions to the dance. I have to admit that Jay and I are impressed. They look real cute while dancing.

We get hungry from all the dancing and play fighting we've been doing, so we order some pizza. The food comes while we're watching Netflix and making out. Kayla has been clinging to me and Christina to Jay ever since we started dancing, so we were able to discern who was interested in who. It's now midnight and Jay motions to Christina to go upstairs with him, but she declines. She claims she has to get home before curfew otherwise, she'll get in trouble. We don't know if she's telling the truth or not, but shortly after that conversation, Kayla and Christina leave. Jay stays about fifteen minutes longer than they do and then he heads home. I clean up the kitchen and living room and then go to sleep.

It's morning and I'm awakened by hunger pains. I don't know why I'm so hungry because I ate shortly before I went to sleep. I walk past my dad's room and stick my head in to see if there's any sign of him. Unfortunately, he's still missing in action. He's been gone for way longer than the three days he said he'd be gone and I haven't heard anything from him. He hasn't called or texted me. I head to the kitchen and fix a bowl of cereal. I was hoping to see him in here cooking breakfast or watching television, but he's not. I'm beginning to think that something is wrong.

While I eat my cereal, I can't put this feeling I'm having out of my mind. My gut is telling me that things just aren't right with my pop. I should call the police and issue a missing person's report. Before I do that, I go upstairs to his room to see if I can find some hotel information. I didn't even think to ask where he was headed, so I hope he has his lodging information somewhere. Although I search through everything, I don't find a single piece of paper pertaining to his travel accommodations.

Maybe he left something in his lab in the basement to lead me in the right direction. I'm not permitted in his lab because there's sensitive information down there, but this is an extenuating circumstance, so I have no choice but to violate my father's no lab policy. I open the lab door and walk down the first three stairs. While I'm walking down the stairs, I hear a car pull into the driveway. It's about time he's home!

I turn around and zoom up the stairs. I close

the door back, so he doesn't know I entered his lab. I'm relieved that he's home. The worry I had was really wearing me down. I feel a great burden lifted off my shoulders now. I run to the front door, but I don't see my dad. To my surprise, I see Dr. Robinson getting out of the car. My dad must have swung a rendezvous with Dr. Robinson and they're just returning. I wonder why he hasn't gotten out of the car.

"Hi, how are you? Dr. Robinson is my dad in the car?" I ask.

"Hello, Nayr. He's not with me. I was hoping he was here with you," Dr. Robinson replies.

She comes inside the house and we sit in the kitchen. I explain to her that I haven't seen my dad, since he left for his business trip weeks ago. Dr. Robinson has a troubled look on her face. Her face clearly expresses that she shares the same concern that I have for my dad's whereabouts. I tell her that we've had no communication at all. She tells me that my dad was supposed to contact her a few days after he left, but neglected to do so.

"When your dad didn't call or text, I started to get concerned. I figured something went wrong with his trip," Dr. Robinson says.

"What could go wrong with a conference?" I ask.

"Your dad's work is a little more than a conference to say the least. It's of the utmost importance. It's revolutionary and purely genius," she shares.

"I know he's a physicist, but that stuff is boring and doesn't seem to be all that important. You make it seem like he's saving mankind or something," I respond.

"Nayr, to some degree he is saving mankind," Dr. Robinson replies. "African American mankind."

I inquire, "What are you talking about? Can you speak clearly without mysteries?"

"I can. It'll be easier to explain in your dad's lab. I'll bring you up to speed and hopefully clear up some concerns you may have. I'll be honest that it's not looking good for what's going on. If he isn't back, we should fear the worst," Dr. Robinson speaks.

We make it to the basement and I'm amazed at the equipment my dad has down here. He's really made extraordinary improvements and upgrades since the last time I stepped foot down here. Now, I see why he stopped letting me come down here. My dad's lab is like a state of the art facility like the ones that are depicted in science fiction movies.

"Wow! My dad really outdid himself down here. I knew he did some work, but I had no idea it looked like this," I utter.

"Yes, his facility is excellent. His research is funded by the university," replies the doctor.

"Yeah, I know. After my mom died, he was going to quit the university and get a job less demanding to be home with me and then the university paid for him to create a lab here at the house, so they wouldn't lose him. He never told me how much they gave him to build the lab though," I explain.

"Right, they knew your dad had an exceptional mind and didn't want to lose him. He's the type of person that a university can build a department around. That's why they made him department head and lets him make decisions," Dr. Robinson voices.

"I know my dad is exceptional at work and at home. He's always been my hero. His integrity is unquestioned and unrivaled," I reply.

"I agree. That's why I decided to keep in contact with him," Dr. Robinson mentions.

I inquire, "So, where is my father and what do you need to explain to me down here for me to understand what's going on? You do know if he's dead that you can just tell me?"

"I don't know if your dad is dead or not, but he very well could be because he should have been back by now. His work was extremely important and dangerous. I hope this isn't upsetting to you. I don't want you to breakdown from this news," Dr. Robinson vocalizes.

I reply, "I won't breakdown. I know I'm young, but my dad raised me into a man. A strong black man at that. He raised me to be thoughtful, responsible, respectful, and meticulous in all that I do. He holds me accountable for my actions and never makes excuses for me if I am slacking. He always told me that a day may come where he wouldn't be by my side, so he prepared me to live my life without him. I just want to know what's going on, so I can process things."

Dr. Robinson begins to tell me about my dad's research. I know that there are many intricate details of my dad's work that I find boring, so I hope there are some aspects of it that I think are interesting.

"Okay, now I'm no expert on your father's work, but he explained some of what he was working on the time I spent the night and also during some of our phone conversations. Your dad was working on teleportation," Dr. Robinson words.

"Is teleportation when you move an object from one place to another without physically touching the object or without the object actually moving the distance to the other location?" I ask.

"Yes, that's exactly it. You have the mind for this just like your father. I guess the apple didn't fall far from the tree," Dr. Robinson compliments.

"Well, I am my father's child, so it's only right that I picked up some of his intellect. I still have a lot to learn though," I remark.

She states, "I see. Must be good genes."

"Yes, ma'am. So is this the teleportation device right here?" I inquire.

"Well, it was supposed to be a teleportation device, but it's a little bit more advanced than that," Dr. Robinson answers.

I solicit, "What could be more advanced than teleportation? Did my dad create a time machine?"

"Nayr, yes. That's precisely what your father created. It's the first time machine known to man. He cracked the code to time travel. He told me in the process of trying to create teleportation, he stumbled onto time travel. He, himself, never thought it possible," Dr. Robinson mentions.

"This is amazing! My father is the man. I just didn't know how much of the man he was until now," I boast.

"He is, but I think his invention may have gotten him into trouble. You see, your dad went back into time to make things right and something could have gone wrong," Dr. Robinson tells.

I communicate, "Now, it makes sense. The first time he went out of town he didn't drive his car, but I just assumed he called a cab or something. Then when he came home, he just popped up seemingly out of thin air. This most recent time, when he left with his colleagues, I left the house minutes before they did, but I forgot my phone, so I came back to get it. It was strange to me that when I got home just a few minutes later to grab it, there was no trace of my dad or any of his business contacts, but his car was still here. Now, I know why."

"They evaporated into thin air, is why," she says.

"Do you know where they were going? What is this dangerous mission you mentioned?" I ask.

"Yes, they went back to Africa during the early stages of the Trans-Atlantic Slave Trade," she responds.

"This is unreal. Africa! That's a very dangerous mission. The Slave Trade is at least the 15th century depending on what time period they went back to," I mention.

The doctor informs, "Your father didn't say what year they were going back to. He only told me because he needed my help. The first time he went to Africa via the time machine, his time travel calculations were off and he ended up in Senegal, but was miles away from his intended destination of the Senegal River. Although, it was an extremely dangerous journey, he made it anyway. The Wolof people inhabit this region of Africa. While there, he met with the king of the Wolofs. They were very kind to your father. From there, he branched out to other leaders from Nigeria, Cameroon, and other coastal countries and formed what they called Slave Trade Opposition Patrol (S.T.O.P.)."

"I guess my dad is a real life hero! He stands by what he's always taught me. I never would have imagined this. I guess nobody could," I interject.

She tells, "Your dad even brought several of the tribe members back to current times, so they could see what was going on in present day. He and his colleagues here in the United States showed them videos of how the Slave Trade oppressed black people for centuries to come. What this did was show some of the willing participants in the Slave Trade that it didn't benefit them to capture tribal men and women and sell them into slavery. They saw first-hand that the white man was not to be trusted.

The doctor states, "Your father told me that while they were here they strategized a plan to thwart the institution of slavery. The major thing they had to do was be sure that they could all communicate to some degree. Your father was the integral part that made the entire plan work. I'm sure you know that your father was well versed in many African languages and now you know why."

"I always wondered why he studied languages that had been extinct for years. He even taught me some of those languages. We would play ancient word games all the time. I used to know them like I knew English. Let me think, in Cameroon they spoke Duli, the people of Guinea spoke Baga Kaloum, and Nigerians spoke Ajawa. My dad had to be planning this for longer than a decade," I narrate.

"Your father told me that this is his life's work,

so yes he's been planning it for a very long time," Dr. Robinson replies. "His colleagues are historic linguists from all over the world. They are the ones who taught him the languages."

"Dr. Robinson, some of those guys used to play the word games with us. We'd play Scrabble in Ancient African languages. I don't know what to say," I comment.

"There's not much to say. I'm still at a loss for words myself. Your dad is a master planner. Each of his colleagues specializes in a particular language, so where he falls short, they can step in. All bases covered, except for whatever has him delayed now," Dr. Robinson reports.

CHAPTER 10
Harry's Perspective

The food has been plentiful over the last few weeks. Fortunately, I've been sleeping quite comfortably while here. I didn't think I'd ever be able to adjust to not having my memory foam mattress under me while I slept, but I was wrong. I don't know if I've gotten used to my current sleeping arrangements or if my mind has just told me that I have to make do with what I have. My African brothers have taught me a tremendous amount about my heritage that has been lost because of the Atlantic Slave Trade.

I feel like I'm at home even though I'm hundreds of years away from what I call home. The only thing I'm missing is my son. I know he's home being responsible, so I'm not worried about that. However, I'm sure he's wondering where I am and why I haven't contacted him again. I should have told him about my invention and my plans to travel back in time. At least he would know where his pop is and probably handle my absence a little better. They say hindsight is twenty-twenty for a reason. I'll make it up to him when we meet again.

We know that the Portuguese sailors will return with intentions to raid Senegal and we are ready for them. We've been training the Wolof people in battle tactics that are used in the twenty first century. I've even had a bit of good fortune. I came across a makeshift storage shed that had many damaged guns in it. Damaged guns were often given to the natives of Africa as payment for slaves, so it doesn't surprise me that these guns are here. We're ahead of the Trans-Atlantic Slave Trade, so these weapons were most likely given to tribe leaders for Africans who were taken back to Portugal to be used as slaves. The good thing is that I was able to fix many of them because they only had minor issues. The white man is very dishonest, so I'm not surprised that the white man would screw Africans on both sides of the deal.

The extra weapons will be invaluable when it comes time to fight. The river means too much for them in terms of the slave trade and the acquisition of gold, so they won't let it go easily. We can't and won't allow the white man to take the river or us as slaves. This is one battle that we can't afford to lose. I'm sure after the butt whooping we gave the Portuguese sailors the first time around, they will return with a vengeance. They also know that we have some of their men held hostage, so they'll definitely be ready to do whatever they have to do to return their comrades safely.

The next day I'm awakened by a sudden rush of screaming people. I jump up and grab my .50 caliber because I'm sure the raid has started. I crouch low and look out of a small peep hole I made, so I wouldn't have to expose myself. I don't see the white man anywhere, but I do see several of the Wolof people who were lookouts for approaching ships running through the village. They are alerting everyone that the Portuguese are coming.

It's funny how I feel like I'm a part of history. This scene unfolding reminds me of American history when Paul Revere warned the colonists that the Redcoats were coming. History will repeat in that we will be victorious today just as the underdog was on the day of Paul Revere's ride. All of the warriors have been prepped on what to do. It will take the Portuguese hours to get up the river valley, so until then… we wait.

One tactical advantage we have is that we can see them coming and they can't fit all of their ships in the canal at once. We have to use this to our advantage. They're not going to be expecting the extra weapons we have either. Fortunately, we didn't sink all of their ships during the initial skirmish because we were able to salvage equipment and weapons that were on them. Many of the natives wanted to enjoy the rum that was on the ships, but I talked them into not indulging in it. As always, I refrained from drinking any of it. Liquor is just one more item in the white man's big bag of poison to feed the black man to rip him and his family apart. I'm not falling for it. I never have and I never will.

Hours pass and finally we see the first ship followed by many more coming down the river. Another shot to defeat the white demonic spirit who enslaved, assaulted, raped, and oppressed my people for centuries. The hair on my arms is standing straight up like needles poking out of my skin from acupuncture. This is the new Independence Day. The ships are within striking distance, so the next phase of the S.T.O.P. mission is about to take place.

The first thing some of our warriors do is begin shooting at the ships as they sail closer. We hope to shoot and kill our opposition, but our main objective is to distract them for a moment. We need their soldiers to be distracted from our fastest and most agile warriors. They are waiting in hiding spots to flash out and hit the first ship with Molotov cocktails. We'll burn the first ship and limit their visibility. With the ship burning they'll never be able to see us in our hiding spots. They'll be forced to abandon ship by jumping into the water.

As planned, the initial shots work amazingly. The Portuguese soldiers fire back on us without realizing that our warriors were shooting the Molotov cocktails from a propulsion device I rigged to give them more distance. There are several direct hits from our team. Some of the Molotov cocktails hit the sides of the ships and begin burning immediately and some even land on the main deck of the ships and begin burning upon impact.

Their men jump off of the ships and into the water to avoid a fiery death. I wonder if they know that they'll be meeting their demise anyway. After the slave raiders jump into the Senegal River, some of them swim towards land, others get overtaken by waves from the ships, and others are thrown a line to climb up from their fellow countrymen. Our men fire upon their men as they climb the ropes. They are easy targets like sitting ducks.

The smoke plumes infiltrate the air and we still have the sight advantage. There's a tremendous amount of gun fire erupting through the air. It's extremely loud to the point where thinking has become difficult. The Portuguese begin to shoot their cannons at us. They must have their best cannon ball shooters this time because it appears that their accuracy is better than the last time. They keep shooting the cannons at us and we're taking casualties again.

I didn't want to use my last RPG, but I have

no choice. This particular ship is causing too much damage to our team, so I get in position and take the shot. The rocket soars through the sky like superman and blows the vessel clear out of the water. It's a direct hit and the ship and its crew are blown to smithereens. Debris sails miles into the sky and I can see the look of disbelief from our soldiers and theirs. That RPG is modern day technology and is like magic to them.

We are taking fewer casualties now that the cannon is down. Our warriors continue to fire upon the ships as they sail closer. Unfortunately, another ship is in range now and has begun to shoot the cannon it has on its deck. The battlefield sounds like a construction site, the super bowl, and a bomb testing site all in one. We keep shooting despite the losses of lives we're taking. The Portuguese are not without injury and death themselves. We are holding our own to be such a small outfit. We are getting what we expected for this is war.

I run into the brush to keep covered from the Portuguese. I find an ideal location to be able to shoot the .50 caliber at the opposition. The noise it makes is extremely loud, so I hope it's not easily heard over all of the other shooting that's going on. I'm shredding their men and their ships and so are my colleagues. Another ship begins to take on water and I can tell it's going down. The battle is tilting in our favor. I taste victory today in my mother country.

Many more of their men are jumping into the water, but most of them keep shooting at us. Even some of their soldiers are involved in hand to hand combat with our soldiers on the shoreline. They are no match for our warriors in hand to hand combat. I can see our men slamming their men to the ground easily. Also, their men don't have the physical attributes to be successful against us in one on one fights. They are fat and sloppy, while our warriors are slim, trim, and spry. I'm elated to see how inept they are against our men.

We'll have this victory in the bag soon. Many of the ships that are furthest from the battleground are empty. I see there are smaller boats with a capacity of maybe eight to ten men per boat have been deployed and are on the shoreline. The only problem is that those boats are empty too. Unfortunately, this means that the white man is on shore and in great numbers. I have to get back to the others to warn them. While on my way back to the others, I see white men infiltrating our fortress. I fire my nine millimeter pistol and shoot one of the devils in the eye as I get closer. Another slave trapper jumps from behind a tree and points his gun at me.

"Drop the gun nigger," he says.

I decide to act like I don't know what he's saying. I give him a look of befuddlement and don't drop my weapon. He speaks again telling me to drop the gun. I throw the gun at his feet and when he looks down at it for a split second I rush him. I wrestle him to the ground with relative ease and take my hunting knife and slice his throat. I see why white men use guns all the time and it's because they can't fight.

I make it back to our main combat site and warn some of our men that we may be under attack from a second wave of the enemy's soldiers, but it's too late. The white men have swarmed around us and we're surrounded. I didn't see this coming at all. I can't believe the table of victory turned on us so quickly. This is why you never count your chickens before they hatch. We continue fighting, but they have us surrounded completely and our men are losing their lives, so we drop our weapons and put our hands in the sky.

"My name is Captain Estevao Afonso and you're now the property of Portugal. We will kill you if you attempt to be belligerent and combative. You will be loaded onto our ships and you will go with us. Please don't make us harm you any more than we already have," he recites.

He's the Portuguese captain who's credited as being the first slave trader to enter the Senegal River. While here, he attempted to kidnap two of the Wolof children from a hut, but was unable to do so because the children's father beat him up. I hate him like I hate hell. I want to wipe that devilish grin off of this bastard's face. He isn't a man; he's a coward because after the beating he took he ran back to his ship and left.

My African brothers and I are disgusted by our current predicament, but there isn't much we can do. Every one of our men, including me, wants to rip Afonso's heart out of his chest and feed it to him. None of our eyes have dropped down in fear. We stare at him longer and harder than two pit bulls about to engage in a dog fight. Clearly, he can tell that we aren't afraid of him.

"It seems that all of you niggers want to stare at me as if you want to harm me. Well, that's never going to happen. I'll show you who's in control of this country now. Portugal is in control and I'm sent in the name of Portugal, so that means I control you. Unfortunately, I have to show you all who's in control, so you won't attack me later," he speaks.

He tells one of his men to string up a rope to a tree and put a boulder by it. His soldier follows his orders, but has one of our warriors move the boulder into positon for him.

"I don't like the way you niggers are looking at me. As if you want to hurt me. I guess I'll just have to make a lesson out of one of you for the rest of you to see that I don't tolerate insubordination," the captain states.

With everyone looking at him while he speaks, Afonso walks up to one of our soldiers and shoots him in both of his eye sockets. His brain matter splatters all over the place even on the captain. I can tell the captain is a savage man because he doesn't even flinch. All of our warriors are visibly shaken by the captain's outright rage and violence. He's a brutal man, but still a coward nonetheless.

Captain Afonso asks as he grabs one warrior by the face, "Who's the leader of your resistance?"

Our warrior doesn't answer probably because he doesn't understand what he's saying. The Portuguese soldiers talk amongst one another briefly. They are about to commit a tactic that's meant to keep everyone in line. Many slave owners would use this torture tactic to make an example out of one slave to show the others what would happen to them if they got out of line. It's a scare tactic that's very harsh, but worked very well. They would often tie a slave up and beat him or her severely. In other instances, they might even rape a male slave to emasculate him and reduce his influence within his family or slave network.

"I think you're the leader. You had the biggest gun and the fancy jacket. Grab the nigger and string him up," Captain Afonso orders.

CHAPTER 11
Nayr's Perspective

"My dad could be over there captured or even possibly dead. I don't know what to do. I can't just sit here doing nothing!" I exclaim.

"There's nothing you can do. They're back in time, so I don't know what to tell you to do. It looks like all we can do is wait," Dr. Robinson verbalizes.

I reply, "I disagree. There has to be something we can do. Maybe we can turn this machine on and travel back to see what's up with my dad and his friends."

"That's a noble cause, but the time travel device only allows for one trip at a time. Once you take a trip, you have to return to the destination you initially departed from. Your dad explained that you can't just jump from place to place and never return to your starting location.

It's like catching a round trip flight there and back," Dr. Robinson explains.

"Darn, that sucks. I feel helpless. I can't even help my pop," I comment.

I ask the doctor to tell me all that she knows about the time machine. She tells me that my dad explained it to her, but some of the stuff was out of her understanding. She informs me that my dad read from his notes while trying to explain the machine.

I ask, "Where are the notes?"

"The notes were locked in a safe hidden over there. He put them back as soon as he finished reading from them," she tells and points across the room.

I rush to the wall and expose the safe. The safe has an eight digit key code. There's no way I can break the code and I have no idea what it is. I enter my dad's birthday, my mom's birthday, and my birthday. I think of all the possibilities of numbers, but none of them open the safe.

It could take forever to open the safe. I definitely don't have forever, so I have to keep trying. What can it be? Come on Dad, tell me something. Maybe I'll never figure it out. Eight digits. Hmm eight digits. What has eight digits and is significant enough for my dad to use?

"I think I figured it out! This is my last option. My mom's departure date to heaven is the only tattoo that my dad has. He never liked tattoos, but he said that was the saddest day of his life.

Come on Dad, please let this be it," I remark.

I enter the numbers that correspond to my mother's going home date. Twelve, twenty three, twenty and fourteen are the numbers I enter and the safe beeps and opens. My dad's notes are right there. I feverishly open the booklet and begin reading.

It says here that the time machine operates by creating a gap between molecules. Molecules are in motion and remain in motion at the same rate unless they're influenced by something. My dad created a basin of particles and then placed magnetic polar dissectors inside of it. It says here that the magnetic polar dissectors pull the particles away from one another.

He describes it in his notes as if someone's running full speed ahead in one direction and then out of nowhere gets snatched by a hook in another direction their path will be slightly or drastically altered in the opposing force's direction depending on the amount of force of the hook. He placed the magnets strategically and equidistant from one another to have the particles moving at the same rate in opposing directions. It says here, that at a level twelve speed and intensity teleportation became possible. He was able to move the average size person twenty feet.

Furthermore, time travel was still unknown to him. According to the notes, he wanted to increase the teleportation distance, so he increased the power and speed of the magnetic polar dissector and saw an unfamiliar and unexpected result. He saw a huge portal that seemed to exist inside the vacuum and looked inside of it. He was able to see flashes of events that he recognized. At that point, he knew what he had.

"I see a formula here that seems to be the last entry in his notes. It pertains to tectonic plate movements. He has some numbers scratched out and others entered," I comment.

"That's not surprising because he had to redo his math on tectonic plate movement. Somehow that tied into time travel for him. Unfortunately, I don't know how," Dr. Robinson states.

"Well, his notes tell how they tie into the equation. Apparently, his findings reveal that the past is constantly running. The past exists as the present does, but it's just not easily accessed," I speak.

"Okay, go on," Dr. Robinson urges.

I verbalize, "It says here that each day the earth rotates, there's a distinct number of particle activity that takes place in the earth's atmosphere. My dad used a particle ferret in conjunction with the time machine. He found a way to detect the amount of atmospheric particle activity on a daily basis. He also determined that each day the earth loses the same amount of particle activity. For example, if the earth has a hundred particle activities today, tomorrow it will only have ninety-nine, and the next day it'll only have ninety-eight. It became a math equation to detect the number of particle activity on any given day."

Now, he could go back in time to any day by using the time machine and the particle ferret. He needed the calculation from me because the latitude and longitude may not put him in the right locations while traveling through time because of the tectonic shift. Continents drift for whatever reasons, so he needed to plug the actual distance from his current location to where he was going.

"I get it. That's how he ended up miles away from where he wanted to be. His figures didn't account for land erosion over the many decades which sent him off target. Well, the good thing is he was able to refine his calculation, so he should have gotten there on target," Dr. Robinson words.

"I guess that's good, but he hasn't made it back safely yet, so it really doesn't matter if he made it there safely or not," I say frankly.

Dr. Robinson takes a step back, rolls her eyes, and pops her neck in response to my comment. I didn't mean to be rude; I was just being matter of fact. I apologize anyway because she is trying to help and it's not right to disrespect my elders. I don't even know how to turn this thing on.

"Dr. Robinson, do you know how to turn this machine on?" I ask.

"I know your father hit a few switches to turn

it on. Those three green buttons are what he used to activate it. You have to hold them down simultaneously for it to work. The only thing is that even if it comes on, you still won't be able to use it because it's a one-way device. Remember, your father will have to come back first," Dr. Robinson reiterates.

"I know, but I at least want to turn it on just to get a feel for the machine. I want to see the way it lights up and the sounds it makes. This is my dad's lifelong project, so I want to know as much about it as possible," I reply.

I press the three green buttons simultaneously and the machine starts making a sound similar to a clothes dryer. The time machine is lit up and sounds like it's fully operational. I look at some of the indicators on the time machine and it displays the destination of the most recent trip. I don't know what all these numbers mean, but the date and time my dad left with his colleagues is next to all of the numbers. This has to be where they went. I turn on the magnets to the machine and they start moving. Unfortunately, no portal opens up as the doctor spoke of.

"I guess it really is only a one-way device. It's really sad that we can't just jump in there and save the day if that's what needs to be done," Dr. Robinson says. "To think about it, there were two rectangular bars that had small slits in them that are no longer here. Maybe they went with your dad."

"I know. This machine doesn't even seem to be working now. It's gonna kill me just waiting and not being able to do anything," I speak.

"I know it will. I know and for what it's worth, it's already eating me up inside. I'm sorry you have to endure this. I know it's tough," the doctor utters.

I grab the book with all of my dad's notes in it and look back through it to hopefully see something that I may have missed the first time. However, my search produces no luck. There's no grand slam in the bottom of the ninth inning to win the World Series. I'm so frustrated that I slam the book down to the floor. The book hits its spine as it comes in contact with the floor. I notice that the spine is severely compromised as I pick the book up. Additionally, I notice that there's a slip of paper inside of the spine.

My eyes get so huge that they almost pop out of their sockets. I grab the paper, open it up, and read it. It's a letter written in my father's handwriting.

I read aloud, "*My son is my life and I will always have his back. When he is weak, I am strong, for I am his spine…. I am his reserve parachute; I am his backup plan.*

I raised my son to care for himself in my absence or when I'm weak, for I know a day will come when I can't help myself. I trust my son will take my teachings and be the family's strength, for in that instance he is my spine. He is my reserve parachute; my son is my backup plan. If my son ever wants to find me, he can always go to the place where we built forts."

I take in every word of the letter. My dad's words are very moving to the point where they bring me to tears. Dr. Robinson gives me a rub on my back. My dad really thinks highly of me. I'm your spine Dad. That's right. I wipe my tears and reflect on the times my dad and I shared over the years.

"That's beautiful. Your father cares for you deeply. He wants you to know that he's always with you even when he's not around," Dr. Robinson says.

I reply, "I know. My dad often told me that I was his backup plan. I'm sorry Dad. I'm not...Wait... Find you... Place where we built forts.... Backup plan."

I bolt out of the lab as if a masked gunman were after me. Dr. Robinson doesn't know why I took off running, but she follows as close behind me as she possibly can. Clearly, she knows the rule about if someone takes off running, you take off running too. According to the rules, you ask questions later when the running has ceased. I run upstairs to the attic and begin a frantic search. I don't know what I'm looking for, but it has to be something and I bet I'll know it when I see it. Dr. Robinson finally catches up to me.

"What's going on Nayr? Can you not take off running like that next time? Can you not make my heart jump out of my chest?" calmly asks Dr.

Robinson.

"I'm sorry ma'am, but something just popped into my head and I had to come check it out. I don't think the letter we found is only a heartfelt plea from my dad. I think it's much more. He was telling me something," I answer while I search.

"Telling you something like what?" Dr. Robinson investigates.

"I don't know yet, but my dad wrote that I can find him in the place we built forts. I think that he's telling me in code to come rescue him and whatever I need to do that is up here. My dad always called me his backup plan," I reply.

"Why up here?" Dr. Robinson solicits.

"It's simple. When I was a kid, my dad and I used to build forts up here. Well, they weren't real forts; they were made out of blankets and strings. He'd have me sneak under them like a snake. I would have to make it to him without being detected. It was always a lot of fun. We'd even have fake campouts up here," I narrate.

"Sounds like your dad was one big kid. That's a special bond you two have. I love to see a man take an interest in his children. We need more of them," she words.

"I'd combine my boy scout skills with the things my dad taught me and I eventually got pretty good at being undetected," I convey.

I keep searching while the doctor and I converse. She eventually joins in the search. I notice a spot in the attic where the insulation looks to be recently disturbed. I walk over to the spot and reach behind the insulation, but I don't feel anything. Fortunately, I look to the floor and I see what looks like two black rectangles. Why would these be back here? Also, why would the key to my dad's weapon collection be sitting here with them?

"Dr. Robinson, what did you say about some black rectangles earlier?" I ask.

"Oh, it's probably nothing, but I was saying that there were two black rectangular blocks with slits in them connected to the time machine when your dad was showing it to me," Dr. Robinson recalls.

The black objects that I'm feasting my eyes on look just like what Dr. Robinson has described. There's no reason for these to be hidden if they're not important. Dad wouldn't leave me a clue to come searching the attic for no reason. Everything my father does is intentional. This is no coincidence.

"Did the black rectangular boxes resemble these?" I ask sarcastically.

"Yes, those look exactly like them," Dr. Robinson replies enthusiastically.

I cradle the black boxes like a mother cradles her newborn baby and walk carefully back to Dad's lab. Dr. Robinson tells me that the boxes were aligned evenly on the two posts on each side of the vacuum portal. I sit each box down vertically according to Dr. Robinson's recollection. We hurry back to the control panel, but it looks exactly the same as it did before. It's doing nothing. It's like the machine is still dead.

I thought we were on to something. What else could be missing? Dr. Robinson claims the setup is exactly as Dad had it. I don't get it. I decide to turn all three buttons back to red and then turn them back to green. This time the machine sounds like a clothes dryer being on, but now there's also a beeping sound and there's an indicator light flashing that wasn't on before.

"I forgot about the beeping sound. The machine was definitely beeping when your dad engaged it!" Dr. Robinson exclaims.

"Great! Now we are getting somewhere. I hope the machine is ready to go because I am. I'm going to get my dad and bring him home," I dictate.

I run to my room to take off my house clothes and put on my military outfit from when we would play paintball. It has endless pockets and something tells me that I'm going to need every single one of them. My suit will provide perfect protection from an untrained eye because it's camouflage in color and it's waterproof. When I get back downstairs, Dr. Robinson is waiting for me. I open my dad's weapon cellar and I immediately see that he's been stocking up ammunition and weapons that I've never seen before.

He has AR-15s, .50 calibers, RPGs, handguns, and many other weapons. I'm like a kid in a candy store right now. I don't know exactly what to grab, but I'm grabbing as much as possible.

"I'm grabbing all of this stuff, but I don't even know what can go through the machine with me," I say.

"Your dad said that you can take what you can carry, but it has to be on you. It can't be sitting on the floor beside you. You have to be physically wearing it or carrying it," Dr. Robinson offers.

"Okay. The time I've been spending in the gym will finally pay off for more than getting girls," I say jokingly.

"Good, well make sure you take the sniper rifle. It has an effective firing range of 800 meters. It doesn't have a lot of recoil either. A nice and clean shot," Dr. Robinson explains.

"I didn't know you knew about guns and shooting," I comment.

"Well, you never asked. I have three brothers and no sisters. Needless to say, I spent a lot of time doing some not so girly things. I was what one would call a tomboy. I wasn't always this pretty. It took years for me to transform into who you see before you today," my dad's love interest verbalizes boastfully.

"It'd be a great help if you came with me," I say.

"Oh, what made you think I wasn't coming?

Why wouldn't I take probably the most important mission ever taken for our ancestors?" Dr. Robinson asks.

"I understand, but you can't wear heels to Africa to save our people. You should go back to the attic and look through a big box sitting to left of the door entrance because it has some of my mom's old clothes in it. I'm sure you'll find that they fit. You look to be her size," I voice.

Doc goes upstairs and looks around for some clothes. She comes back with my mother's paintball outfit on and her boots. She looks very militant. I'm glad to have another person going with me. We'll have double the weapons and double the brain power. She loads up on ammunition and weapons just as I have. We carry guns and backpacks filled with water, food, and other supplies with us too. We're ready for time travel.

"We need to figure out how to set the timer for the machine to engage," I say.

"There's a dial off to the left of the panel that you can set. That's how your dad was able to send himself and his friends," replies the doctor.

"We have to go through at the same time because we only get one-way trips. At least we'll be there as a duo and can locate my dad," I say.

I'm set to go and then I realize that there's one major problem. The time machine's dial is set to detect the particle activity on the day he left. If we don't change the dial, we'll end up going to the same day he went to a few weeks ago. That'll put us three weeks behind his current location. He could be anywhere in three weeks. I wonder if we should switch the dial.

I ask, "Do you think we should change the dial to try to get us closer to the three weeks that my dad has been gone?"

"I do. Having all of the figures makes it a simple math equation. It'll take me no time to put the numbers together and reset the dial. Also, if we go back at the same time or before the time your dad and his friends left, we may not find him because they technically wouldn't have left yet. Again, if we set it for the three weeks he's been gone, we know he's there. I'm still floored that your dad made a backup time travel box," Dr. Robinson speaks.

"Okay, so he's been gone for exactly 22 days, so set the dial for 21 days. We'll find him from there," I order.

Dr. Robinson states, "The only problem with any day be arrive back in time is that we don't know what day your father got stuck. For that matter we don't even know if he's stuck at all."

"I agree. That's the problem we'll face with any day we choose to go back to, so we'll just have to live with what we pick," I comment.

Dr. Robinson sets the dial to reflect what I told her. We have all of our gear, weapons, and food supplies. We set the timer and jump into the time machine.

Countdown.... 59...58...57...56...

CHAPTER 12
Nayr's Perspective

We make it through the time travel machine and end up in a wooded area with high brushes. I don't know for sure where we are, but it's extremely hot. I wish there were street signs like back home for us to be able to tell where we are for sure. We are sweating profusely from the heat and it doesn't help any that we have on all of this gear.

"Dr. Robinson, are you alright? You feel okay?" I inquire.

"Yes, Nayr. I'm fine. I just felt like I was riding on an extremely high and fast roller coaster ride. It was exhilarating and fun," she replies.

I reply, "I know what you mean. I felt like I was on the top of a train while it was zooming through a tunnel. I agree, it was definitely thrilling."

"Why does the fun stuff always have to be so short lived?" Dr. Robinson asks.

I respond, "I don't know why it's like that, but it surely is. Now, is the hard part. We have to find my dad."

"I know we do. I just wish we knew which direction to head in. Hell, we don't even know for certain where we are," Dr. Robinson says.

"Yeah, it's quite the conundrum, but we'll persevere. We have to have faith. I suggest that we head this way. I don't know why, but we have to head somewhere," I comment.

The doc agrees with me for us to head in the direction I suggested. We wander for hours without bumping into any people. We know now that we're definitely in Africa because the doctor recognizes certain geographical features that are specific to the region. I agree with her because of the heat and some of the animals we've seen remind me of an episode of national geographic pertaining to Africa.

Night falls on us, so we decide to stop searching for my dad tonight. We are both pretty tired too because we've been roaming around in the heat all day carrying gear. We pull down some bushes and make pallets out of them. I put down animal repellent around our resting area to keep any harmful animals away. I even drop a set of flashing lights because they have been known to repel lions. I also string some bells on wires and surround our fortress. Hopefully, if we have an intruder, the bells will alert us before they're on top of us. We rest in the pitch black forest as we'll call it. The sounds we hear as we rest are out of this world.

Dr. Robinson is freaking out from all of the noises we're hearing. Quite the contrary, I'm fine with the sounds of the wilderness. Being out here reminds me of the times when my dad and I would go camping in Pennsylvania and New York. All of the noises sound similar to one another and actually bring a warm feeling over me because they remind me of my dad.

I did find it interesting to see all of the African wildlife face to face. Until today, I had only seen ostriches, grebes, and pelicans on National Geographic. It's like I'm living history. I need to shut my mind off and go to sleep. I'm sure I'll need to be well rested to endure tomorrow's navigating. I'll see if I can sleep with one eye open just in case some wildlife attempts to eat us.

The next morning I'm awaked by the heat of the sun on my face. I have to say that I'm shocked that I slept so well under these circumstances. I was out cold, so much for sleeping with one eye open. I really was exhausted. The sun's intensity manages to creep under my eyelids with its brightness. I look around and my heart suddenly drops to my stomach. To my horror, there's no trace of Dr. Robinson.

Where is she? I know she didn't get dragged away by an animal while I slept unsuspectingly. All of her gear is right here before me, but there's no trace of her. I jump up and look around the immediate area. I'm reluctant to call her name because that may alert potential slave catchers or a hungry pack of lions to my location. I see something move in the brush, but I can't see exactly what it is because the sun is shining directly in my face.

I drop to the ground to use the cover of the brush as my friend and to get the sun out of my eyes. I sliver over to my pallet and grab my nine millimeter pistol. I make sure the silencer is on tightly and I crouch down in firing position. I don't want to hurt anyone, but if it comes down to being either me or someone else, it'll be someone else. The person is definitely coming this way, but little does he or she know that I'm ready. I'm ready to pounce at a second's notice and take the person down.

To my anguish, I hear something approaching me from behind. Unfortunately, I can't see over the brush to make out who or what is approaching me. I pull out another nine millimeter pistol and stay crouched low and out of sight. I have both arms fully out stretched with both guns cocked and ready to be fired in the directions of the unknown parties. I peer through the brush back and forth scrutinizing any and everything.

Finally, I have a stroke of good luck. The brush blows in the right direction and allows me to see through it. I spot Dr. Robinson approaching our campsite from the left. I stay in a crouched position and move toward Dr. Robinson to the left while keeping my eye on whatever is moving in on us from the right. I grab Dr. Robinson to the ground and cover her mouth so she doesn't make any noise.

I lie parallel to the ground with both guns aimed. The perpetrator is now revealed. I see the perpetrator's face clearly from about ten feet away, but I don't fire. I don't fire because it's an animal that is approaching us. The doctor recognizes the animal as a banded mongoose. Uncharacteristically, the mongoose is alone, but it appears to be fairly young, so maybe it wandered away from the group.

Dr. Robinson picks up the cub and plays with it. I'm not in the mood for playing, so I tell Dr. Robinson it's time we get moving. She wants to take the mongoose with us. I don't have a problem with it. I just know we have to move quickly. We pack up our campsite and grab our gear. We begin walking and I realize something that could help us dearly.

"We've seen a great white pelicans and grebes. That tells me two things and they both should be vital information," I say.

"Really? What's that?" Dr. Robinson asks.

I communicate, "From what I remember,

great white pelicans and grebes are both native birds to Senegal, Africa. Also, the great white pelican is a freshwater bird, so the Senegal River has to be near. It wouldn't venture too far away from the body of water it drinks from."

"Right, that's great! We know where we are now. We can build on that to further our progress," the doctor expresses.

"Exactly, let's put two and two together. We know from history that the Portuguese set up a slave trade network on the Senegal River, so it's likely that my dad went to the Senegal River to thwart slavery there. It's what I would do. We need to get there," I explain.

"That's a great idea, but how will we find it?" Dr. Robinson asks.

"We'll just follow the birds. We'll walk in the direction they're flocking to. Hopefully, that'll lead us to where we need to be," I voice.

We have our gear on and we make our way in the direction of the birds. The further we walk, the more bugs I notice are around. The increased presence of bugs lets me know that we're nearing a body of water. I'm hoping it's the Senegal River. Next, we begin to hear the sounds of flowing water. We hear waves splashing as we get closer and closer. We now can faintly see men in the distance and can clearly make out Portuguese flags draped on ships in the water. We see black and white men. Unfortunately, the white men are holding guns and the black men aren't.

They have one man tied up and dangling from a makeshift hanging post. All of the men with guns pointed at the black men are making the other black men look directly at the strung up black man. There's a single white man standing on the platform in front of where the black man is raised. The black man who's strung up is without his pants, underwear, or shoes. The black man, to my surprise, is wearing the same style army jacket as me. Those jackets were not made during this time period. To my horror, I realize that it's my dad's jacket. Oh my goodness, that's my dad hanging there! That white demon is about to kill my father or already has. I haven't seen my dad move at all since we've been watching.

I wish we were closer so I could get a better shot, but I have to do what I have to do. I take my sniper rifle off of my shoulder, get in position, and fire a single round at the white man standing in front of my father. Fortunately, the noise of the river muffles the sound of the gunshot. However, my shot is not accurate. Instead, of hitting the white man, the bullet sails well over his head and nobody detects that a shot was even fired. I'm disappointed in myself because I missed and there isn't even any wind to blame it on. I move a few feet closer, but remain in cover, so I can get a better shot.

The next thing that happens nearly kills me. The white man reaches down and swipes something in front of my father. All I see is blood spewing on the ground below where my dad is tied up. Next, the white man bends down and picks up something from the ground. He stuffs whatever it is in my dad's mouth. My dad's back is to me, but I realize that he cut my dad's testicles or penis off and placed them or it in his mouth. All of the other black men who are looking at what's transpiring look broken and hurt. They can no longer look at what's going on.

My heart has just been ripped out of my chest at this moment. My father has been murdered in front of me and I missed the shot that could have kept him alive. We've come all this way to get him home safely and I blew it. I've let my dad, myself, and my loving mother down. I know she's looking down on me shaking her head.

"I'm sorry Nayr. I know this is a crushing blow. To be so close and not reach your desired outcome can be discouraging, but remember that you can finish your father's life's work. We are here and you have to finish it," Dr. Robinson encourages.

"Dr. Robinson, you're right. I am his spine. I am his backup plan. They think they cut off the head of the snake, but little do they know... The snake has two heads. We have to continue his dream," I reply.

"That's right. Let me know what you want to do," Dr. Robinson says. "I'm loaded and ready to shoot on your order."

"Wait, let's not be so quick to use force and be irrational. My dad, God rest his soul, would always tell me that being irrational clouds one's judgment. We should use our heads and I have a plan," I vocalize.

The doc replies, "I'm all ears. Just let me know."

First, I tell Dr. Robinson to hand me the mongoose. Secondly, I ask Dr. Robinson to go to another position to be ready to shoot the men who have guns drawn on the black people. Next, I take some strings and tie them to the mongoose's feet. After that, I attach bells to the strings. I stay hidden in the brush and gently put the mongoose down. Dr. Robinson's in position and the decoy is ready to be released.

We attack now. We move swiftly, decisively, and precisely.

CHAPTER 13
Nayr's Perspective

I pat the mongoose on the back and it takes off running. Seconds later, the bells begin jingling as the animal scampers about. I change my position by crawling in the opposite direction of the mongoose. The demonic slave traders are distracted by the sound of the bells and the movement it's producing in the bushes. As planned, their soldiers are distracted.

Fortunately, Dr. Robinson follows the plan to perfection. She begins shooting the soldiers holding guns to our people. I was skeptical about the doctor's shooting abilities, but she proves me wrong. She hits every white man she shoots at without missing. Her aim is flawless and she puts bullets from the sniper rifle in each of our enemies' heads. I also shoot from a sniper's position and have many kill shots.

Their men are falling left and right. Skulls of the Portuguese men are being obliterated. Brains and blood fly through the air like dust when a building is imploded. They think the shots are coming from where the mongoose is running and where the sound of bells chime, so they open fire on its location. We continue shooting their men as they shoot at a phantom intruder. As guns begin to fall out of the hands of the men we've killed, our men grab the guns and shoot at the Portuguese. In a few short minutes, we have control of the port and all of the Portuguese soldiers.

Since everything's in order, I come from my hiding position. I didn't want to give up my position prematurely and risk the chance of another wave of Portuguese soldiers popping up on us out of nowhere. I see Dr. Robinson sprinting from her position at one hundred miles per hour. I look behind her to see if she's being chased, but nothing or no one is trailing her. I'm clueless as to what her problem is, so I scream her name, but she's focused and doesn't respond.

While I'm screaming her name, I hear something I've heard hundreds, no thousands of times in my lifetime. I hear someone in a voice that sounds eerily familiar to my father's voice calling my name. I turn my body and eyes to the direction of the voice and to my surprise, delight, and confusion I see my dad racing towards me. Obviously, Dr. Robinson spotted my dad from her position. I smile the hugest smile I've ever given in my life and race towards my dad. I meet my father, my hero, and we share the best father-son embrace that we've ever had.

Eventually, Dr. Robinson makes it to our hug site and joins in our celebration. We laugh and rejoice while we embrace. Dr. Robinson sheds tears while we hug. My father wipes the tears from her eyes and then rubs her gently. I'm still in utter disbelief about what has transpired.

"Dad, we thought you were dead. We saw that man mutilate you. I was devastated," I utter.

"Son, you obviously didn't see me get mutilated. Not wearing that jacket may have saved my life. Look over there at where my comrade Craig was murdered. We go back many years. That would have been me if I were wearing that camouflage jacket," Dad says.

"Well, what happened?" Dr. Robinson inquires.

"The raid came so fast today that I never had a chance to get fully dressed. I barely had time to put on my pants and grab my gun before all hell broke loose, so that's why I'm not in full battle gear. The guy you saw get mutilated is my colleague Craig from the United States. He was on patrol last night and asked to wear my jacket, so he could carry more items, so I obliged. Captain Afonso mistook him for being the leader of our resistance because of the jacket. They'll never understand that we're all equal. There's no hierarchy here. He was a great man, friend, and soldier," my father narrates.

"I'm sorry for the loss of your friend. He had to be a good man if he was willing to risk it all and travel back in history to battle for freedom," Dr. Robinson comments.

"Yes, he was an excellent person all the way around. Craig will be sorely missed by all. All of our fallen warriors will be missed, but it's a part of war. Death is a part of life and we must all embrace it," my dad states.

We turn our attention to the Portuguese men that we've captured. They are all kneeling down in front of us with their hands behind their heads. Members of S.T.O.P. have them under their control at gunpoint, so they can't escape. While the Portuguese men are being detained, some of our team gain access to their ships and raid them for supplies. We find guns, gunpowder, fabrics and many other goods that we can use. We also find many slave restraints in the under decks of the ships. This area of the ships would be where they would store slaves during the Middle Passage.

I can't believe that I'm standing in an actual ship of slavery. It's a very sobering experience. I'm elated by the fact that we were able to keep slaves from being transported in the treacherous conditions of the Middle Passage. I've seen many videos that depicted how tight and uncomfortable the Middle Passage was, but I never expected it to be as bad as it is down here. I'm becoming angry just thinking about the conditions my ancestors suffered.

We unload the slave restraints from the ship and take them to the shoreline. All of the Portuguese soldiers are shackled and chained in slave restraints. It's very ironic that the chains that were brought to this country to restrain us are now being used to imprison the very people who brought them here. The Portuguese soldiers are now prisoners of war. I find my father after we secure all of the white men.

"Dad, everything's secured. We've offloaded the ships' contents and chained up all of the white invaders. They are discontent with the entire situation. That's for sure," I say.

"Great son! I knew you'd take care of things for us. I have to admit that I'm not as young as I used to be. All of this has really worn me out. I need time to rest because my body is extremely sore," Dad reports.

"I know Dad. You're getting up there in age. This is a young man's war. You can just be part of the think tank and not part of the physical combat," I joke.

"Yeah, your old man is really your old man. Maybe only being the brains isn't such a bad idea, but I could never be that guy. I've always been hands on with everything I do. You know that son," Dad remarks.

I respond, "I didn't think you would, but I

figured I'd at least throw it out there. I'm glad you are hands on with everything including fatherhood."

"That means a lot son. Well, since we're going down this line of conversation, I'm glad you came to save me. I knew if I told you outright to come save me, you'd come without hesitation. I was secretive and mysterious about things because I wanted to leave things in the hands of fate. I told myself that if you found and figured out the clues I left behind then it had to be destined for you to come save me. My son is my backup plan," Dad orates.

"Dad, I wasn't going to rest until I made it over here. I didn't know how I was gonna do it. I just knew it would happen. Now, I'm here and everything went according to plan," I state.

"Right, you made it and saved the day. The distraction with the bells was a classic move. Very strategic if I do say so myself. You did well son. No, very well," says Dad.

"Thanks Dad. You know you've trained me very well from all the years of camping, hunting, paintball, and various other activities," I voice.

Dad remarks, "It was all part of the plan son. I never wanted you to have to come to rescue me, but my time travel vehicle broke down on me, so I was unable return. I did want you to be thoroughly trained just in case the unthinkable happened."

"It worked because I felt like I was prepared

for everything that was happening," I reply.

My dad and I continue to converse. He tells me about how his invention can never be known to too many people because of its power. He fears that if his technology falls into the wrong hands, it'll be trouble for the world. Dad even states that he contemplates destroying the machines and all of his data pertaining to them. I understand his position on why he wants to destroy his machines, but there are also pros to keeping them intact. We discuss many pros to keeping the machines up and running, but Dad doesn't come to any conclusions at this point.

The next thing we discuss is what we're going to do while here. My dad explains that we have a lot more work to do. One of the things he wants to do is build up the continent. Knowing what he knows about the future of Africa he hopes to start building it up now. He knows that it'll take a tremendous amount of time and effort to accomplish, but he feels it can be done. My father informs me that our efforts to build Africa up will ensure that it becomes the world power it was intended to be before slavery raped it of its people and resources.

CHAPTER 14
Harry's Perspective

It's been a week here in Senegal since we defeated the Portuguese soldiers and took them into custody. I estimate that they'll be sending more ships soon to navigate the African coast to get slaves or to find out what happened to the ships they sent to rescue the soldiers we captured during the first battle. Thankfully, I was able to repair the time machine that was damaged and we are beyond ready for battle. Nayr, Dr. Robinson, and I have visited the present day several times to restock our shelves for battle here. Unfortunately, we are only able to get weapons and other small supplies to Senegal because of the size of the time travel portal. The good thing is between the items we confiscated from the Portuguese ships and what we brought from present day we were able to arm a vast majority of our warriors.

I feel badly about how I was able to get my hands on the weapons, but I find solace in the fact that they'll be used for a good cause. I explained to Nayr that these are unusual circumstances and sometimes drastic situations call for drastic measures. He understands that we have to have certain things to win the battle, so he's not taken back by my actions. I've been using the teleportation aspect of my creation to put myself in military installations and stealing their weapons. No other options are available to get the weapons we need.

I've been enjoying the Senegal cuisine, but I'm also glad that I was able to get home and have a home cooked meal. I was definitely missing the modern day amenities such as air conditioning, indoor plumbing, and refrigeration. With that being said, I'm back here in Senegal and ready to deploy. I'm risking my life all over again and giving up the comforts afforded to me in the present day. I couldn't be more proud than I am at this moment because my son is beside me. He's a stellar young man. Dr. Robinson also decided to stay along with the fight and we appreciate her assistance.

We need some of the white prisoners to do some labor in Senegal, so we put them to work. They're building tunnels from the Senegal River to serve as waterways for irrigation to other areas. This is a daunting task and will need many more laborers to get this job completed as expeditiously as possible. We will also need several prisoners to sail with us to Portugal. A few of these men are captains, so their expertise is valued and needed.

The other men are going to help us when we get to Portugal. We are stopping at the port city of Lagos. That's where an overwhelming amount of slave trading took place. Captain Afonso and other captains are disgusted at their current predicament, so they negotiate their release upon getting back to Lagos. That's fine with us because we need their help as badly as they want to be released.

We load the ships with the necessities for our mission. Next, we embark the ships and prepare for departure. We depart Senegal and head north towards Lagos. As we sail, we can't help but notice how calm the sea is. It's almost like the seas are calm just for us. Even the captains of the ships comment on how uncharacteristically passive the coastal waters are. On the way up the coast, we see two ships that belong to Great Britain. We shoot one of them up and allow the other ship to get away. We send a few men to jump on board the British ship we attacked and take what we could salvage to use on our journey.

Although, the boat ride is quite comfortable and the weather is enjoyable, most of our warriors are down below the main deck. That's not how we want it to be, but we know that it'll be strange if we're seen sailing up the coast with Africans having a party on the upper deck. They're not traveling in the same horrid conditions that the Middle Passage normally afforded. The warriors who are on deck appear to be shackled, but they aren't. Their hands are free to grab their weapons to fire on the white prisoners if they try to rebel.

We eventually arrive in Lagos. We have the white men under heavy guard to ensure they don't signal to their countrymen that something is awry. I'm below the main deck on one ship listening to one of the leaders give his men a speech about being successful today. I can comprehend a vast majority of his speech and I'm able to fill in the rest to get the gist of it all. All of the ships are under the same protocol. The African leaders are informing their men of what to do.

We anchor the ships and now it's time to strike. The ramps used to unload and load the ship's cargo are now in place. We run from under the main deck and strike swiftly, precisely, and convincingly. There are many people on the port in hopes of acquiring slaves, but we don't know which ones are armed and which ones aren't, so we fire on everyone. This attack is similar to the Trojan Horse attack used in Troy.

The plan works perfectly too. Within hours, the port city of Lagos is ours. As A part of the deal we had with Captain Afonso, he is to take us to King Henry's location. He takes us near Sagres to Vila do Infante and we raid Henry's village. We have no problem winning this gunfight because our weapons and training have afforded us the edge. Not to mention, King Henry's guards are caught totally by surprise.

The rest of our soldiers have gone to other port cities such as Lisbon and Porto and carried out attacks there too. Within days, we have taken control of the small country of Portugal. The kingdom has been taken and most of the citizens of Portugal don't put up any resistance. There are a few small pockets of resistance, but nothing to worry about.

The warriors on our team begin to act out of character because they're angry from all of the deaths the Portuguese have caused. Unfortunately, the warriors decide to decimate Portugal. They take any goods they find useful and burn down whatever they deem useless. We have thousands of troops at various locations in Portugal. We have to thank the Portuguese slave traders for their expertise in packing the ships extremely tight with cargo. The leaders of the Wolof people decide that they are going to export the Portuguese people back to Senegal to help with the newfound need for laborers.

The African leaders threaten the lives of the captains and their families if they don't sail the white slaves back to Africa. They happily oblige and within days of being in Portugal, white slaves are loaded into the lower decks of the ships to begin their new lives in Africa. It's amazing to me to bear witness to history changing before my eyes. Five ships depart Lagos with a total of sixteen hundred slaves and head to Senegal to help with labor that we know the continent needs to thrive in the future. Other ships depart from Lisbon and Porto carrying thousands of slaves as well.

The white slaves suffer the same atrocities as black slaves did during the Middle Passage. They are cramped into small spaces that don't allow for them to stretch or anything. Many of them become sick and die from disease during transport. Some of the Wolof leaders even beat the white men because they hoist fecal matter at them. The good thing is that it doesn't take many men to help transport the slaves to Africa because of the superior planning and advanced weaponry we have.

The ships return to Africa and the Wolof people store the white people in slave quarters. They're housed in the slave quarters until they can be divided and sent to various locations in Africa. Unfortunately, things get completely out of control when the whites are being divided. Several white men overpower some of the Wolof people and even kill them. One of the Wolof people who's murdered is a ten year old girl. The skirmish is quick and the Wolof people regain control of things. However, the Wolof people don't take the little girl's murder lightly and are livid. They decide that being civil to the white people is no longer an option because he is truly the devil. They begin to torture and kill the Portuguese people as retaliation for the African girl's murder. One warrior is dragging a white man through the streets because he wants to see how fast his skin will begin to burn off. Additionally, in the first few nights, many of the white women are raped over and over by our warriors. Many of them have never seen white people before, so they are intrigued by the differences between them and us.

Some of the white female slaves are even victims of sodomy. The Wolof leaders support their warriors' actions because they feel it's payback for the white man's violence and also indulge in the same behavior. Many Portuguese men are forced to watch black men have orgies with their wives, sisters, and mothers. Unfortunately, the torture doesn't stop there. The warriors begin to have competitions to see who could come up with the most creative methods of torture. One man named Rodrigo refuses to change his name to one more consistent with the Wolof names and a warrior cuts his foot off and shoves it up his ass. I never intended for this to happen, but it's out of my control. I'm not the leader of this outfit and I have my son and Dr. Robinson to take care of.

Not too long after the ships with the white

slaves depart from Portugal, they return with empty hulls looking for more cargo. Fortunately, there's plenty of it. More Portuguese men, women, and children are sent to Africa as part of the workforce. Also, the ships return with more African warriors who are ready to fight. They're immediately armed and prepped for battle. Portugal is decimated and looks like a third world country. It has been looted for its goods and resources with much more looting to come.

CHAPTER 15
Harry's Perspective

I know we need to get things tamed in Portugal to ensure we are ready for our upcoming battle, so I call a meeting with all of the leaders. I tell them that our next battle is near and that we need to get all of the warriors settled down and focused. The leaders are very serious about battle and being successful, so they corral their troops and get them ready. They actually go further than I anticipate and implement curfews and a no rum policy for the next few days. That's the dedication we need to achieve our desired result. We see ships coming from the direction of England.

"Son, are you prepared for the events that are soon to take place?" I ask.

"Yes, I'm ready. I'm mentally and physically ready. In fact, I've never been more ready for anything in my life," Nayr answers.

"Great, I'm honored to fight with you. Son, you're my hero. I've always been proud of you for being able to stay focused after your mom died. That could have broken you, but it didn't. We've been through adversity many times and I wouldn't want any other person beside me today. Remember, be swift, precise, and clear headed. No emotions and use your head as you always do," I orate.

"I got it Dad. I'm your reserve parachute and you're mine. Dad, you were my spine when mom passed and you've never let me down. You're the consummate definition of a man and of a father. Thank you for showing me how a man should conduct himself," Nayr returns.

"Those ships will be here soon. They'll empty all of the ship's artillery on us before they come on shore, so you know not to be near the shoreline. We'll let them blow their load and then they'll approach to try to gain control on land. This is mainly the Wolof's war, so let them have it. We'll provide as much backup as they need which shouldn't be much. Stay with me and Dr. Robinson and we'll use the RPGs to take out some of the ships. We don't need to endanger ourselves when we don't have to," I narrate.

The British have their ships along the coast of Lagos and begin firing heavily. We have Portuguese men on the shoreline firing back on the British. We are using them as decoys. The

Portuguese soldiers are shooting at the British on our orders because their families' lives depend on it. Many of them are being killed from the British assault. We use the Portuguese soldiers as distractions to what's really going on. I know if the British soldiers saw a bunch of black men fighting on the coast of Portugal, they would think it was crazy, so we are doing it this way.

As the British fleet destroys the coastline killing Portuguese soldiers, many of the remaining Portuguese soldiers retreat as directed by me. The act of retreating makes the British think they've won and therefore they come on shore. Everything's going according to plan. Things work so well that I never have to fire the RPG. Many British soldiers come on shore while others stay on the ships firing as cover. To their surprise, they are met by Africans who begin firing upon them. Fortunately for us, many British soldiers are killed on the shore while trying to infiltrate Portugal.

A few ships are approaching the battlefield from the south which surprises many. The ships are toting the British flag on its sails and the British fleet thinks reinforcements have arrived from some of their countrymen who have been on slave voyages, but they are wrong. To the British's surprise, they start taking on fire from the very ships they thought were their allies. I'm not shocked that the British are confused because we draped the Portuguese ships that we commandeered in British sails. We placed them in the ocean off the coastline as a tactical advantage for when the British showed up. The thought was that they would see the sails and think they were friendlies. Even though they are taking heavy fire, the British continue fighting. The battle is going on longer than expected, so Nayr is forced to use the RPG and is accurate the one time he uses it. He blows up three of their ships with only one use of the RPG. The ships being so close together allowed him to take out multiple ships with only one firing.

The battling ends as soon as the three ships blow up in a single instance. The British see how dominant we are, so they wave the white flag and turn their guns down and cannons away from us, so we aren't compelled to think they still want to battle. Our African warriors empty the British ships of their soldiers one by one. The British are totally surprised by how many black people they see and are bewildered as to how we are in control. They don't know that a few of us can speak English, so they speak freely.

"How did the niggers invade Portugal and get ships and guns?" one British soldier asks another.

"I was thinking the same thing myself. Hell, it'll be weeks before any other ships come looking for us. This was supposed to be quick and easy. Too bad we didn't bring more ships," answers the soldier.

"His highness is going to hang these black

niggers by the balls and rape their wives," another British soldier chimes in.

I respond, "Your king will do nothing of the sort. He'll be captured right along with you and the rest of your men. Bet you're wondering how a black man speaks more intelligently than you. Yes, black men are educated because we are kings."

The expressions of anger and confusion on their faces are priceless. It feels so good to have impeded the progress of the two leading slave trading countries that being Portugal and Britain respectively. Who would have ever thought it possible? Hours later, we have the men off of their ships and onto the Portuguese vessels. The Wolof people send them to the Senegal River to be used as workers in that region or in other areas of Africa. Africa has a lot of land that needs to be worked and built up and now the Africans realize it. The workforce to help with that endeavor is now available. I can already see where this is going and it is bizarre, but exciting.

"Nayr, you are a pretty nice shot with that RPG. You normally hear people say they killed two birds with one stone and you upped the deal. You killed three birds with one stone. I think I was more amazed than the British soldiers were," I say.

"It was a lucky shot. I was aiming for the ship to the left," Nayr replies jokingly.

"We served them the business. This is a

great victory for us. The people of Africa can rest comfortably tonight. We all deserve a round of applause," I speak.

Dr. Robinson states, "It is a great victory. Your invention and your superior battle strategy have made this moment possible. We thank you."

"We all played an integral part in this victory. We couldn't have done this without the help of the Wolof people. Their leaders allowed me to enter the zone and educate them on what was coming. I'm proud to be a black man more now than ever. I'm proud to stand and fight with my ancestors," I recite.

"You're right. All members of S.T.O.P. made this possible and we should all rejoice in this moment. Shucks, I know I am," Nayr voices. "I almost want to take a drink."

"Son, let's not go that far, but I understand what you mean. You're still underage, so no rum for you. That stuff is the devil's poison anyway. You don't need it," I utter. "Besides, we still have more battling to do. This isn't over for us. We are almost to the end, but we still have to cut the head off of the snake. Until then, we're in jeopardy. Keep a sharp mind because this will be the most arduous battle we've encountered to this day."

"Dad, what are you talking about? What else could be next after taking on the British? Portugal and Britain are the major players in the slave trade right?" Nayr asks.

I answer, "Yes, they are the major players in the slave trade. I know we've defeated the Portuguese with relative ease and we control their country now, so we don't have to worry about them. The English battle is an entirely different animal. We've only scratched the surface when it comes to defeating them. They are large, they are fierce, and they are formidable adversaries. We have to take the next step and take over England as we have done Portugal. If we do that, then we can rest and really celebrate a victory. Look at it like this son, it's like we're the Eastern Conference Champions in the NBA and now we have to face the Western Conference Champions to win it all. Our victory today is like us leading in game one of the NBA Finals by one point at the end of the first quarter. I'm basically saying that there's no need to celebrate and we have a lot more work to do."

"I understand what you mean, but this is one cumbersome task. Like you said, they're mighty. We should draw them out again and bring them back to the coast. We'll have them right where we want them. Dad, they'll surrender again and then we can celebrate for real. We can pop bottles like the NBA players do when they win the championship. Don't be mad at me for mentioning the champagne because I was just continuing your analogy," Nayr says.

"Right, there will be no champagne for you

and you're a little off on your plan of having the English come back here. The thing is that we have to take the fight to them before they even know they have lost here on the shores of Portugal. The reason I ordered one of their ships destroyed and let the other one go unharmed when our soldiers were in the Portuguese ships was because I needed them to think Portugal was responsible. The main reason for doing that was because I wanted to weaken their infrastructure. We were able to destroy many of their ships and take some of their men. Now, we have control of their ships. They've been hurt badly, so now we can invade their country," I explain.

Dr. Robinson asks, "Do we really have to do this? Is it really necessary? Can't we take what we've done here and build on it gradually?"

"Dad, I agree with Dr. Robinson. We should be able to chill for a little bit. We've made great progress here. Dad, look at it like this... The English ships are either destroyed or we have control of them, so we have time to relax. They can't even sail with as much zeal as they once did," voices Nayr.

"Son, have you ever seen a professional boxing match? Have you ever watched one and paid close attention?" I ask.

"Of course Dad. You know we've watched several of them together. I always scrutinize the entire fight," Nayr answers.

"I know you do. When a boxer has his

opponent dazed and weak, he doesn't let him off the hook. Instead, he keeps his assault going until his opponent can no longer fight. If he were to back off when the opponent was only weak, it's possible for the weak party to regain strength and potentially win the fight. In battle, you always have to take advantage of the upper hand when it's afforded to you," I narrate.

"Good point! I didn't look at it like that. It makes sense to seize an opportunity when it comes your way," speaks Dr. Robinson.

"Follow me for a second as I narrate. In the movie the Godfather, there's a character named Sollozzo who wants another character named Don Vito Corleone to make a deal with him, but Don Vito doesn't accept the deal. Sollozzo is upset by Don Vito's refusal to do business with him, so he attempts to kill him, but it doesn't work. Later in the movie, Don Vito's son, Michael Corleone speaks on the situation. He says Sollozzo won't stop attempting to kill Don Vito because Don Vito's death is vital to Sollozzo making the deal he initially proposed to Don Vito. Michael Corleone is adamant about killing Sollozzo because he knows as long as Sollozzo is alive, he'll be gunning for Don Vito Corleone," I dictate as they listen.

"Dad, not to be rude, but an old gangster movie has nothing to do with what we have going on here today. I don't get the point of the story you just told," Nayr comments.

"Son, you're wise in so many ways, but this concept went way over your head. I'll clarify things for you. The Atlantic Slave Trade was an extremely horrible and crippling system for Africans and for the continent of Africa. Millions upon millions of Africans were enslaved, tortured, and killed as we are all well aware. Now, the Atlantic Slave Trade was the extreme opposite for the English. They experienced wealth and prosperity beyond our wildest dreams because of the slave trade. The money they made would probably estimate into the trillions of dollars.

Once they saw how financially lucrative the institution of slavery was for Portugal, the British had to get involved. I tell you the story about the Godfather movie because it speaks about intent. Once something or someone is intent on a mission, the only way to stop them is to kill them. Son, the English are intent on the slave trade and will stop at nothing to have it because the British king knows what it means for their financial stability present and future. If we don't finish what we've started here, they'll just rebuild to be better and stronger. We can't take the chance of what we've done being done in vain.

Now, I can't and won't even attempt to force you to fight the British with me, but the warriors and I are going to. We know what it takes to reach our desired outcome, so we are putting in the work for that to happen. I'd love to have you two with me, but I understand if you don't want to go because my fight is not necessarily your fight. I respect your decisions one way or the other as I hope you respect my decision to make this last journey in the name of freedom," I recite.

"Wow, I guess I still have a lot to learn about life. I thought I had it all figured out, but clearly I don't. Dad, I'm going with you and the others. I always have your back. I'll be on the same ship as you when we sail to England," Nayr conveys.

Dr. Robinson chimes in, "Don't forget about me. I'll be on the ship as well. As the young people say 'Ride or Die'. That's me all the way."

"Great! I'm glad you two are coming," I say.

The ships we took control of are ready to go. The warriors, at the behest of their leaders, have been prepping the ships for us to go. We are going to use the same strategy we used to infiltrate the Portuguese's shoreline. We'll have white men on the deck looking as if they have control of things, but they won't. Instead, S.T.O.P. will be running the show. We've bribed the British captains of the vessels just as we did the Portuguese captains. They are totally under our thumbs and in our pockets.

The day to set sail has arrived. We leave Portugal and head to England. We depart Portugal later than the other ships because we aren't headed to the exact locations. We have British ships and we also have Portuguese ships that are outfitted with British sails to help conceal the ships' true identity. Nayr, Dr. Robinson, and I are on the ship that's a part of the fleet going to London. The other ships are heading to Liverpool and Bristol. These are all integral port cities that we need to have control of. It will take us different amounts of time to arrive at our destinations. Since that is the case, we have to delay our attacks to allow for the others to get into position. We don't want to attack at different times and tip the monarchy off to a battle.

The captains know how long it'll take to get to each port city, so we add an extra day onto that time before we attack. Each fleet is to attack at first sun up on the eighth day of travel. Again, we've been blessed with a calm sea and great weather. We are all in great spirits and are optimistic about the future. We are near London, but it's not time for our synchronized attack, but I have a better idea that may help our fight go more smoothly. I need to talk to the captain about what I want him to do. As I approach the captain of the ship, my son intervenes and tells me he needs to talk to me about something urgent.

"Dad, do you have a minute?" Nayr asks.

"Yes, I do son. Let's step over here to talk privately. Whatever is on your mind seems urgent," I voice.

We walk away from the others, so we can speak in confidence. Nayr has a menacing look on his face and the tone of his voice is definitely filled with concern. I hope I'm able to disarm what issues are troubling him. He needs to have a clear mind when entering into battle. Clear thoughts will help him perform better.

"Dad, we're headed to Britain to thwart slavery. Now, the idea of this is troubling to me on a couple of different fronts. I can't wrap my mind around it, so I want to bring it to you," Nayr speaks.

"What's bothering you son? You do know I'm always here to help you through anything that's bothering you?" I ask.

Nayr answers, "Yes, I do, so here it is. We know that Britain transported millions of slaves over a few hundred years. You told me while I was growing up that our last name of Smith is actually an English name. That means that our ancestors were purchased in America by someone from Britain. Now, if we go further with our plan to conquer the British, it's possible that we may kill the ancestors of the very people who carried our kin to America or kill the ancestors of the person who purchased our ancestors in America. It seems like to me that we'll be changing history, so certain people will never exist and then that makes it possible for us to never exist. We'll be erased from existence possibly. That's frightening to me."

"Your concerns are warranted and I hope I can put your concerns to rest with what I'm going to tell you. Yes, our last name stems from England, so it's likely that our ancestors were owned by a family of English decent. Chances are, the people who owned our ancestors were blacksmiths. They potentially worked in metals making horseshoes or even worked with gold or silver. That's the reason there are so many variations of the last name Smith. I will speak to that first. We, in America, haven't been living our legacy. We've been living the legacy of whoever purchased our ancestors. We carry their family name and make it great. Every accomplishment we make is under the name of someone who oppressed our people. We don't know our real legacy because it has been erased. Our legacy was stopped, interrupted, diverted, or whatever you want to call it whenever the white man kidnapped our ancestors from Africa. Don't be confused son; what we are doing here is not altering history. The truth of what we are doing here is correcting history or at least getting things equal," I explain.

"I understand Dad," Nayr says.

I narrate, "Now, I want to address the second portion of your concerns. You are concerned about whether we will cease to exist because certain people who helped create our future may be killed, never exist or just end up in a totally different place. You have another valid concern and I see you are a deep thinker like your father. I think back to Dr. King when he marched for civil rights. He wasn't concerned about what might happen to him in the future because he was doing what was right at that moment. Dr. King didn't let fear of the unknown preclude him from his mission. That's how we need to proceed. We need to proceed like Harriet Tubman did when she risked her life and directed many slaves to freedom. We have a mission to complete that's for the betterment of our people, so we have to do it even if it means the death or non-existence of us. We cannot waiver or falter in our mission."

"Basically, we may have to sacrifice for others as they have sacrificed for us," Nayr remarks.

"Not basically what we have to do, that's precisely what we have to do. Dr. King and many others risked it all to make the world a better place for us. They jeopardized themselves and their families to open doors for us. Now, it's our time. Dr. King in the 'Mountaintop Speech' pretty much predicted his death, but he forged forward to conquer adversity and prejudice. This fight against slavery is much bigger than you and I. If we end the Atlantic Slave Trade before it begins, we will save millions of people. We'll estimate that ten million Africans were sold into slavery and of course that impacted the lives of millions more in Africa and in the Americas. Africa suffered as a continent because it was stripped of its resources, its men were no longer on the continent to defend it from intruders, and the men were no longer there to help reproduce. The family structure was broken due to slavery. Additionally, the slave trade also impacted the Native Americans. They too lost their identity, they too were stripped of their land, and they too were viciously murdered. The Native Americans lost millions upon millions of their people from the violence waged against them from the white man. The white man has to be stopped at all costs. If that means my life, I am willing to give it," I orate.

Nayr picks his head up and has that troubled look wiped off of his face. He seems more confident about what rests ahead of us. He understands that this quest is bigger than us. It's about righting a wronged ship. He walks off after I tell him to prepare for the plan that I've put together and I approach the captain of our ship.

"Captain, our ship is going to dock early. I want you to take me to King Henry when we dock. I know you hold close council with him, so make it happen. You'll act like I'm a king from Africa and I want to set up a deal to afford him access to a tremendous gold treasure. You'll inform him that I can make the process easy and avoid unnecessary bloodshed," I order.

The captain acquiesces and we arrive in London. My son is with us and is in a vented crate that has our weapons in it. We have other warriors with us who are supposed to be samples of the types of slaves I can also provide to Britain. I have chosen our biggest and most physically attractive soldiers to take with us. I have my nine millimeter pistol with me the entire time. We are escorted to Windsor Castle in Berkshire County by horse drawn carriage. The travel to Windsor Castle is not very far and is just a few miles west of London.

We arrive at the castle and are swiftly taken to King Henry. The British Captain tells him of my fictitious plans to give him gold and slaves and he's all for it. While we talk, I hear gunshots that resemble that of a .50 caliber weapon and I hear grenades exploding. I know my son is out of the crate and is making his move. The king is startled by the noise. I pull out my gun and shoot two of his guards dead. I point my gun at King Henry and take him hostage in his own palace.

The "slave samples" we brought with us are now armed and they are involved in a gunfight with the king's soldiers. The weapons we have are too much for their soldiers to compete with. I walk out with Henry and threaten him with death if he doesn't order his men to drop their weapons. Henry is hesitant at first, but eventually sees the predicament he and his men are in, so he tells them to lower their weapons. The castle is now ours. I order King Henry to tell his people that the castle is not to be disturbed for the rest of the night because I don't want anyone to get wind of the fact that we've taken control of the castle. After thinking about it, I felt it would be better for us strategically to gain control of the castle before the attacks from the ships took place.

The next day is the day for our planned attacks. The sun is rising and all hell is breaking loose. We can hear explosions from where we are in the castle. We know our men are winning the battle. London is eventually overtaken by our warriors and many of them make it to Windsor Castle as initially intended. Fortunately, Dr. Robinson is one of the people who makes it here. Hours later, we receive word that Liverpool and Bristol are also under heavy fire. We head to London, so Henry can see the damage done to it.

"Henry, if you value the lives of your subjects, send out word to your men to stop fighting and surrender. Tell them the fight is over," I say.

The amount of damage done to London is unimaginable to him. He looks down to the ground and asks if we can let his most trusted officials deliver the bad news to the rest of his troops, under armed guard of course. There are already hundreds of troops being detained by our warriors. The British regime has fallen to the people of Africa.

Three days later, our warriors with the help of some white prisoners, are escorted to Glasgow. Glasgow is a major ship building center, so we have to utilize it. There will be plenty more ships being built here in the near future. We'll need more ships to transport goods back to Africa. Our men also go to Birmingham, which is one of their largest steel and iron producing centers and take control of it too.

CHAPTER 16
Harry's Perspective

Months have passed since the British have fallen. The situation here is beginning to look a lot like how Portugal looked. Our soldiers haven't forgotten the image of one of our soldiers getting his testicles cut off and stuffed in his mouth, so they continue to mimic the same horrible acts. Warriors are raping white women in front of their husbands knowing the husbands can't do a thing about it. A lot of white men have sold their souls to the Africans. They want to help force other white people to come to Africa to help build the continent up. Slave ships are leaving London, Bristol, and Liverpool regularly. Only this time, the ships are leaving full of cargo and the cargo is white men, women, and children.

Britain no longer looks like it used to. The buildings have been toppled and more and more people are being kidnapped and taken to Africa. The land has suffered tremendously from being burned. We decide to go back to Africa because conditions in Britain are unbearable. Many Africans stay to help facilitate the slave transportations. When we arrive back to the Senegal River basin, things look totally different. The region is already looking like a more established country.

White men are fast at work. They are cutting down trees and building houses. Lumber is being exported to other regions in Africa. Not only is Senegal benefiting from our victory in war, so is Sierra Leone, Nigeria, Morocco, and many of the other African countries. White people are being sold all over the country. The import of slaves has even eliminated the fighting going on amongst the different tribes.

The women and children are given easier jobs than the men, but they still work twelve hour days. There's a lot that goes into building an infrastructure, so the more help the better. Some of the African leaders are more vicious than others. The vicious ones don't cut the white people any slack. I witnessed one leader rip a white man's eyes out because he stared at him for too long. The leader took it as a sign of aggression and an act of disrespect, so he taught him a lesson.

The white slaves are whipped on a daily basis. The conditions are harsh for them here in Africa.

They have to walk very long distances to get to their work sites. Unfortunately, many of them don't make it to their intended work destinations because the African inland has many diseases that they can't overcome. Eventually, horses are taken from Britain and brought to Africa, to help transport the slaves, but there aren't nearly enough horses to completely solve the problem.

Many slaves get out of line, so the Wolof people create a punishment system for the British and Portuguese. One punishment for the white slaves is called horse kicking. Whenever slaves misbehave, some leaders tie them to posts with their arms behind their backs. Next, they place a horse in front of the tied up slave and then make the horse buck by tickling the horse's stomach with a prickly weed. The slave behind the horse bears the brunt of the impact. Many times, the slaves become disfigured or die.

The Wolofs caught two slaves trying to escape this morning and have just decided their fates. Both fates are horrific. After being severely beaten, one is tied up and stood against a wall. Harnessed in front of where he's standing is a thirty foot tree with the branches removed. The tree is cut loose from the harness and swings into the slave and smashes him flat against the wall. It kind of reminds me of a bingo card with the ink blotter. They have a myriad of punishment tactics they employ.

I call the other tactic they use on the other

slave the sling shot. This one also involves using trees to inflict punishment. They tie a rope around the neck of the slave and then tie the rope to a tree branch. The next thing they do is cut the tree down from the opposite direction that she's standing. The tree starts falling and then violently snatches her off of the ground while throwing her in the direction the tree is falling. Her neck is snapped immediately.

It sucks to be a slave and I'm glad that I'm on the better side of it. I guess I'm responsible for things being the way they are, but I'm okay with that. The white men have no rights. Additionally, they have no say so in anything that happens to them or their family. Some slave owners allow the families to stay intact because it's better leverage if the slave thinks about getting out of line. The black slave owner can always threaten the slave's child if he or she wants the slave to obey orders.

As time goes on, I start seeing white women give birth to mixed babies. This drives the white men crazy because they are helpless. They have no way of keeping this from happening and they feel like they let their white pride down. Many of the babies are cared for by the women in the area. The white women in many cases aren't even being raped by the Africans. They are desirous of the strong and well-endowed black men. Their physiques are godlike, so how can anyone resist them?

Water systems are being implanted, fabrics are being made, and mining is being done. Africa is thriving as it was destined to do before the Trans-Atlantic Slave Trade came into existence and crippled it. It's a beautiful sight to see and I'm glad I'm witnessing it firsthand. My son is seeing it with me and he's proud too. Dr. Robinson is taken back by some of the governing methods going on, but overall she's happy about the current situation of Africa. It's better to be them than to be us.

CHAPTER 17
Harry's Perspective

It's funny to me that I haven't used my invention to travel back to present day in months. I would think by now my curiosity about how things were impacted from us taking down Britain and Portugal would have gotten the best of me and influenced me to travel through time to see, but it hasn't. I know it's because things are great here in Africa. I feel like I'm home which is an unfamiliar sensation for me. Even though I was born and raised in America, it never felt like home to me. I always felt like I was a visitor in someone else's home.

I didn't feel at one with myself as I do here in the motherland of Africa. I have no history in The United States of America. My wife is deceased and my son is here with me, so there's nothing left for me there. On the other hand, I can find all the information about how my ancestors really lived because I'm here experiencing it firsthand. Unfortunately, my son is homesick. He's adjusting to life in Africa, but it's hard for him. Nayr misses the modern day amenities that he's grown accustomed to. I totally understand the culture shock that he's experiencing.

I wish there was something I could do to help him feel better. In an attempt, to make Nayr's stay here better, I decide to have the slaves build Nayr, Dr. Robinson, and me a smaller version of the pyramids in Giza. Our home will be made of limestone, but that is no easy task. We have to import the limestone from the Giza plateau. We use the free labor of the British and Portuguese slaves to acquire the limestone. The walk is long and horrific for the whites. A lot of them are expiring from disease while others are perishing from the back breaking work of dragging the limestone for miles to where we are going to have our pyramid built.

In some instances, the slaves even commit suicide by owner. They misbehave and refuse to work to the point where their owners have to kill them to show the others that insubordination isn't acceptable. The good thing is that there are thousands upon thousands of white slaves, so they don't worry about sacrificing a few white people to make their point. As I sit in my chair and watch them retrieve the limestone, I see a stone come flying toward me. Luckily, I see the limestone rock sailing in my direction, so I duck and keep it from hitting me. Although it doesn't hit me, I am still quite angry due to the level of insubordination and the attempt to harm me. I see the direction the stone was thrown from, so I have one of our men approach the slaves in that area. I'm too tired to engage in disciplinary activities.

"Which one of you white chazzers threw that stone at me?" Ken inquires.

Nobody answers him. Additionally, they all act like it never happened. They clearly think that this is a game, but it's not. He knows a lesson has to be taught here and he's the one to teach it. Ken motions two more of our men who also oversee the slaves to assist him in his investigation and interrogation. They come to his aid immediately with guns drawn.

"Grab that chazzer for me and put his hand forward," one of them orders.

My assistants grab the white pig and drag him to the forefront for all to see. The slave resists, so they have no choice but to whip him. They give him several lashes on his back, legs, and even face. His skin has opens up like someone slashed him with a razor several times. Blood is all over his body and he's screaming in pain. Everyone can obviously see that the whipping is causing excruciating pain. I want to step in, but I refrain because discipline is in the hands of the Wolof people. Besides, this type of treatment is what they intended to do to my ancestors when they left Portugal and Britain and sailed down the African coast.

"Now that I have your attention, we can have this conversation again. I know you all understand me clearly because we speak the same language for the most part. Now, someone tell me who threw that stone at me. Being forthcoming will save us a lot of time and you a lot of pain," Ken says to the slaves.

He gets the same response as he did the first time he asked who threw the stone at me. Nobody wants to share what they know, so he has to take the investigation one step further. Ken grabs his bin of salt and pours it on the wounds of the slave who we just beat. He squeals uncontrollably and my men crack up laughing. He's on the ground going into convulsions. I guess the salt in the wounds is worse than the actual wounds.

His screams are hurting everyone's ears and they wish he'd stop making all of that noise. They decide to put him out of his misery and fire one shot to the back of his head. Brain matter splatters all over the place. The slaves look away in horror. My guys pull another slave to the forefront. They ask this slave directly if he knows who threw the stone at me, but he refuses to answer all together.

"Oh, let me guess, you can't talk, huh? Are

you a silent cracker or something?" Ken asks angrily.

The slave speaks, "I speak, but you're a nigger and niggers are beneath me. I'm a duke and I feel no need to answer to a peasant. You're an animal nigger."

"A duke of what? Do you not recognize where you are? A duke means nothing to me. I'm glad you think you're above me, but the way it looks right now is that I'm higher on the hierarchy than you are. You don't have to talk to me. I promise you that it doesn't hurt my feelings," Ken comments. "It's quite troubling to me that you don't respect me and would call me a nigger."

All of the white slaves have devilish grins on their faces from their fellow countryman calling me a nigger. I think they think he's going to get away with it, but he's not. My worker gives him three lashes with the whip and he hollers violently. He falls to the ground in pain. Two guys hold him down, so he can't move. While his mouth is open and he's screaming, Ken takes his knife out of its holster, grabs his tongue, and cuts it off. Blood spews everywhere. The slave's face is entirely covered in blood as his tongue bleeds profusely.

"Now, he can't talk. This is what happens when you disrespect an authority figure. I didn't want to do it, but as you all saw, he forced me to do it. Someone better step up and admit what he's done before I ask again," Ken states.

Finally, someone comes forward and takes ownership for having thrown the stone. The funny thing is that I don't know if the person who has come forward is even the person who threw it. It seems more likely that someone came forward just to stop the torturing of everyone else. It doesn't matter to me one bit who did it, but what does matter to me is that these slaves get in line with the rules. It's not in our best interest to have them thinking they have power. I strive to keep them respectful, but the Wolofs desire to keep them fearful and broken. The slave who threw the stone at me has to pay in their opinion. They have two other slaves hoist an eighty pound limestone boulder in the air and drop it on the slave's legs repeatedly. The slave's legs are broken in several different places and he can't walk. I'm willing to bet that these slaves won't be throwing any more rocks at me. Next, Kens decides to put him out his misery and let the dogs eat him alive.

We've been traveling from getting limestone all day and it's getting dark. Fortunately, we come upon a plantation house that's made out of wood. The slaves built a house for Bama Deli, who was a member of the initial fight against Portugal. He allows me and my men to stay at his plantation house for the night. I leave my slaves chained up outside for the night while I rest comfortably inside. They'll be fine because they're animals anyway.

Bama Deli asks, "Do you want some wine or rum?"

"No, I'm fine, but my men may want to partake. I just want to relax. It's been a very long day to say the least," I reply.

"I see. I know what will help you relax. I have just the thing for you. Come to the back room," Bama Deli says.

When I get to the back room, I see several beds. I'm glad he brought me back here because I just want to sleep until the morning. However, this is not a room for sleeping. This is a comfort room that's meant for having sex with women. The African slave owners use this room to entertain guests when they come to visit. I walk out of the room and Bama Deli follows me.

"You said you want to relax, so I figured the comfort room would work for you," Bama Deli says.

I state, "No, that's not the relaxing I want to do. I really just want to sleep. No more... No less..."

"I'm sorry my friend. I misunderstood what you were saying. Everyone who stops by wants to go to the comfort room to relax with the comfort girls," Bama Deli speaks.

My two men decide to go the comfort room for the night. I go upstairs and get undressed in a bedroom that has been set up for guests. There's a lot of noise coming from downstairs. The comfort room is full of action, but I fall asleep as soon as my head hits the pillow.

The next morning I wake up fully rested. There's breakfast waiting for me downstairs. I get downstairs and my men are already eating breakfast that the slaves have prepared. English muffins are on the table. I crack up laughing over the hilarity of the English slaves serving english muffins. My men tell me about their night.

"You missed a great night," one of my men says.

"That's a matter of opinion. All depends on what one calls a great night," I say.

"Well, we fucked those white bitches all night. They really did comfort us," one of my men says as he laughs.

My other buddy chimes in, "We were at it all night. At one point, I was having sex with three of the comfort girls at the same time. They are nasty beings and loved every minute of it!"

"I'm glad you enjoyed the night. Sleep was good enough for me. My sleeping arrangements suited me just fine," I reply.

One man says, "I slept fine too. I was stretched all over that bed."

"How? Didn't you have the comfort girls with you all night?" I ask.

"Yes, that's the funny part. They slept on the floor on a mat just like dogs do. I would snap my fingers when I wanted them to comfort me and then when I was done with them, I'd literally kick them out of the bed back onto the mat. You know you can't let them sleep in the bed with you. They smell like wet dogs and chicken," he answers.

After breakfast, we go outside and retrieve the slaves. They are still chained where we left them. We throw them some leftovers from breakfast and give them some water to drink. They pick up their stones and we head back to my pyramid's building site.

CHAPTER 18
Nayr's Perspective

Ten years have gone by and I can't believe how fast time flew. There have been many changes to Africa over the years. I can still tell it's Africa, but it looks different from how it did when I first got here. There's a lot less forest and empty plateaus and a lot more buildings. Villages with huts have now been replaced with villages of wooden structures. The work that the slaves have done on the irrigation canals is priceless because Africans now have clean water and that will reduce disease throughout the continent.

Slaves aren't being brought to Africa at an extremely high rate anymore because we have plenty of them here. However, it still seems like I see more and more white people every day. I remember when this first started that many Africans had never seen a white person and now it's common. Nobody even bats an eye now because they are working all over the place. There are plenty of laborers on the continent and things are really being developed. One great benefit of this new workforce is that it has ended all of the warring between different tribes. The white man is unable to manipulate the Africans and pit them against one another. Africa is in harmony within itself as it was intended to be. We're optimistic that in the future we'll be able to release the white people back to their native lands.

Many of our slaves are skilled tradesmen and we use this to our benefit. For example, they are ship makers, steel workers, seamstresses, and welders just to name a few. The slaves work for us and produce goods that we use to trade with other countries. Free labor and knowledge allow Africa to become a world trade center. Our gold and diamonds are protected from foreigners, but we do trade some of it to acquire things that Africa doesn't provide naturally. The progressive thought that I have and knowing what inventions have come about in the future skyrockets Africa centuries head. I guess being from the future has its benefits.

I call a meeting for us to decide how we can further the slave trade and the use of slaves. There are so many of them that we can spare to get rid of some. From the meeting, we determine that we will send the white slaves to what we know as the United States. There is no need to let the slaves get off without working hard every day. Thirty days after our meeting to determine the fate of our subjects, we send ships of white slaves to what is present day United States of America. We know from history that there are many uses for a labor force in the Americas.

I personally take the trip to the Americas to talk to the Powhatan natives. They need to know that at no point is the white man to be trusted because he will take the Powhatan's kindness for weakness. Also, they need to know that the white man will commit acts of genocide on the Powhatan people and other Native American tribes to try to eliminate their existence. We hope to implement a new slave trade that involves white people as the labor force. We believe that this operation with the Powhatan's will really help build up the Americas for the natives. The white man will be the minority in the 'New World'.

The trip across the Atlantic Ocean is pleasant for me. We have many comforts that the white man didn't have during the initial Atlantic Slave Trade. We have ships that are far more advanced than the ones used by the British and Portuguese. We make the trip across the Atlantic in half the time it took them to make it. The Middle Passage is just as brutal for the white slaves as it was for African slaves. No matter how big and fat slaves are, we still cramp them into the same four foot spaces that were originally designed for Africans.

We don't think they mind the horrible transportation conditions, since they saw it fit for our people to travel this way.

We are a week into the voyage to the Americas and decide to give the slaves an opportunity to exercise. They are all on the upper deck of the ship dancing to African Tribal tunes. I walk among them as they dance and I am immediately taken back. Besides the fact that they are all off beat and have no rhythm, their smell is nauseating. I bunch of white people sweating produces a smell that's similar to wet chicken and bologna. I pinch my nose shut as I walk between them. One slave in particular is staring me in the eyes.

"Do you have a problem with your eyes boy?" I ask.

"No, I don't, but I do have a problem with niggers. You're a nigger, so that means that I have a problem with you and the rest of these niggers," the slave replies arrogantly.

"Well, there are no niggers here on this ship. You heathens are sorely mistaken. For you are not in the presence of niggas, monkeys, or any other animal. You are in the presence of kings. You are to refer to us as negus!" I assert.

The slave rolls his eyes and spits at my feet. He's clearly defiant and disrespectful. Every time I look at the slaves' faces, I see the police officer who threw me to the ground and I see the ones who killed Josh in Bridgewater. This slave's attitude is just like those cops' demeanor and it disgusts me. I have a solution to his problem.

"Since you stated that you have a problem with niggers and there are no niggers here, that means you really do have a problem with your eyes. Since we own you, we have to take care of our property," I voice.

I have two of our men chain him flat on his back to a restraint we have on the main deck. The slave fights back when they initially grab him, but he's severely beaten for his resistance. By the time he's chained to the deck, he has little fight left in him.

I speak, "This is what happens when you devils are insubordinate. You'll be chained, whipped, and tortured. Maybe even killed. The choice is yours."

I reach into my pocket and pull out my razor. I raise it in the air for all the slaves to see. I want all of their attention on me as I teach this slave a lesson. They are all focused on what I'm doing.

"Now, this bastard here has a problem with his eyes, so I'm gonna fix that for him. This could be any one of you if you get out of line," I state.

I kneel down over the chained man. He's wiggling and trying to break free from the restraints, but his efforts are to no avail. I take the razor and begin to cut off his left eyelid. Blood runs down his face and into his hair staining it crimson. The powerless slave screams and shakes as I continue with my incisions. His peers look away in horror and utter disbelief. Many of the women regurgitate from the sight of what's happening. Our men don't flinch. In fact, some of them laugh as I finally get his eyelid completely off.

I repeat the same action with the second eyelid as I did with the first. They all scream in horror, but I don't care. Those are the exact same screams Josh had on that terrible night. He didn't deserve what happened to him. Many people will say that these slaves don't deserve what I'm doing to them but who cares. Maybe it's not right what I'm doing, but it damn sure makes us even. I'm not done with my torture tactics. The slave's cries are starting to subside, so I know the pain is starting to settle with his body, but this next move will surely cause his squeals to commence all over again.

To the slave's detriment, I take a handful of salt and dump it on his left and right eyes. His body starts shaking and rattling upon the first drop of salt hitting his eyes. I know it burns like hell. The female slaves start crying louder than they were before. One of the white women slaves jumps up and runs to be by the chained slave's side. I slap her down before she makes it to him. I stand over her as she whimpers in fear.

I reach down and grab her by the throat and say, "I did not order you to move peasant. You move only when I tell you to move."

I kick her in the stomach and she hollers in pain from the blow. The slave with no eyelids is screaming so loudly that I'm sure he can be heard back on the shores of Africa. He's really starting to give me a headache and I can't bare the noise anymore.

"You want some water for your eyes?" I ask.

"Yes, I do," he answers in a very weak voice.

"Yes, what?" I inquire.

"Yes, Master, I do want some water for my eyes," he verbalizes.

I orate, "Now, that's respect. This is the level of respect that we will have going forward. When you address us, you address us as Master because we are your masters. Now, everybody say master on the count of three."

I count out to three and all of the slaves call out master in unison. I love the sound of this. I ask one of our men to get some water. He comes back with a bucket of water and hands it to me. Next, my soldier unchains the slave. The slave makes it to his feet and I tell him the water is over here. He follows the sound of my voice because his visibility is dramatically impaired. As he gets closer to me, I grab him by his belt buckle and throw him off the ship and into the Atlantic Ocean. He is quickly swallowed up by the sea. Next, I grab the female slave who attempted to aid him and throw her off the ship too.

"Help him now bitch. See if you can help him now. I'll gladly get rid of the rest of you too.

You are all property that was free, so it means nothing to discard you like the rodents that you are," I say.

Their exercise time is over, so we escort them back below the deck to the slave quarters. I believe that I have all of their attention now. My men and I go back on the main deck after we secure the slaves and enjoy more of the calm sea. I eventually fall into a deep sleep as we sail the ocean blue. An hour into my sleep, I'm awakened by my soldiers because one of the slaves won't stop screaming. They tell me the slave won't stop making noise until he sees me.

I go below deck to where the slaves are being held and investigate the situation. It smells like a vat of throw up down here. Many of the slaves are covered in urine and fecal matter, so I'll be quick. My soldier points me in the direction of the slave who's screaming out of control. I walk up on him.

"What's your problem boy?" I ask.

"Master, I'm over six feet tall and I'm cramped into a space that's only four feet long. My legs are going numb from being so cramped up. I just want to be moved to the space I was in when I first got loaded onto the ship. I was able to stretch out a little more," he explains.

"I see your dilemma, but I don't know why you thought to have me awakened out of my sleep to keep you from being inconvenienced. That's disrespectful in my opinion. I hope you don't think that you're more important than me," I vocalize.

He replies, "Oh no Master. I know you're more important than I am. I just hoped that you'd be willing to help out because you are so understanding."

"Yes, I am understanding, but I need my rest too. Ordering you slaves around is no easy task. However, I will help you out of your situation. I'll be right back," I say.

I go back to the main deck and come right back to the slave in need. I unchain his legs and he immediately stretches them out to gain some relief from being cramped up. He even lets out a sigh of satisfaction. The slave thanks me for my kind heartedness. As he thanks me, I take my ax from my belt and chop both of his legs off at his knees. Blood gushes all over the place, even splashing the other slaves. The slave screams out of control and is going into convulsions. I pick up his legs and place them near his upper torso and I head back to the deck to finish my nap.

"Do not interrupt my sleep for anything or you'll meet the same fate as him. Don't test my will because you will lose every time!" I yell.

He'll eventually bleed out and the screaming will stop. The other slaves will calm down and be quiet eventually. Three days later we arrive in what we in present day call United States. The weather is fairly warm, so we figure that it must be spring time and not to mention that the trees and flowers appear to be blooming. Shortly after we arrive, we set up a camp site and wait on the natives to approach us.

It's several days later after we've set up a camp and we're surrounded by hundreds of Powhatan Indians. My men immediately grab their weapons just in case they have to defend us. Although they have us surrounded, it doesn't appear that they wish to harm us. It's almost as if they're surrounding us in an observatory fashion. I'd be interested in seeing who we are if I were them too. We have to be like aliens to them. I order our men to put their weapons down. There is no need to cause a bloodbath over a misunderstanding.

We can easily decimate them with our weapons if we have to. We have snipers positioned around our camp to take out the Powhatans if things don't go as planned. Our weapons are down by our sides and the Natives seem to appreciate that the threat of violence is minimum for now. One of the Powhatans calls out to us. He must be the chief because of the way he's dressed. He's an elderly gentleman and is highly decorated.

He says, "Cawaassough. Pyas."

When he says Cawaassough, I immediately raise my hand and greet him. I assume that he's asking for the person who speaks on behalf of our men because that word means talker or orator and Pyas means come here. Fortunately, my father anticipated coming to the western world after he took over Great Britain and Portugal, so he brought a book of Native American words with him. I stumbled upon it, so I began to study the words in it. I hope I'm fluent enough to effectively communicate with the Powhatan people. They inhabit this region of the United States that would be Virginia.

The chief is shocked that I know the language of his people. I tell him that we come in peace and bring him and his people valuable information about the white man. I'm only able to speak in broken phrases and fragments and I'm only able to catch a few words of what he says. Most of them are unintelligible for me.

The chief says, "Wingapo. Apis."

I sit down as he orders me to do. He wants to talk about why we are here and expresses more concern about the valuable information I have for him. The language barrier is a cumbersome task to overcome, but I'm doing my best. He asks me my name and I respond.

"Nuturuwins Nayr," I answer.

As we talk more, I inform him that the white man is dangerous. I tell him the white man is "Reapoke." He immediately takes notice to such a violent charge because that word means devil in the Algonquian language. My father even had the foresight to include pictures of the white men committing acts of genocide. He wants the natives to know exactly what to be prepared for in the event the white man ever approaches them.

I show him the pictures and tap on them as I say, "Reapoke and Wop-poshaumosh."

That means white devil. We converse for several hours about how his people along with the other Native American tribes were slaughtered at the hands of the white man. He promises to spread the word to other tribes to help prevent their extinction. Once we're on one accord and the chief realizes that we come in peace, I send my men to the ship to retrieve several of the slaves. The slaves are a gift from us to them. We don't want any money or goods from them. We just want to help the natives live in peace. My men bring the slaves to the camp site while they are chained up. I turn over most of the slaves we transported to the chief. I have to keep some of them to work on the ship on the voyage back to Africa.

In the future, we want to have the native's land as a place for Africans to live and vacation. We know the value of having the Native Americans as our allies and we also know the value of having access to the vast resources the United States has to offer. I know that the United States is rich in oil and gold that won't be discovered for hundreds of years. We can use a white workforce to help pull those items out of the earth. We have plenty of white slaves who can be used here for work. This is just another step in helping to keep Africa great.

We stay in the native's land for another two weeks. It's now time for us to depart and head back to our country. We've done our part in warning the Powhatan people of the white man's true intentions and have even given them slaves to help ease their workload. For now, we have done all we can do. We sail back to Africa and have no major interruptions. We return to Africa to a hero's welcome. Our people are flourishing and relishing the economic boom that Africa is experiencing. I enjoy the Mother Country fully and keep exporting slaves to the United States of America. When the time is right, we'll go back across the Atlantic to begin our business there. Until then, we'll wait.

EPILOGUE

I didn't mind leaving Africa for a little a while because the trip to America was necessary. I knew there wouldn't be any disturbances while I was gone because we're heavily protected here. Since the tribes are unified and have weapons, they are able to defend themselves from foreign invaders. Our shoreline is defended by our superior fighting allegiance. We've had several more battles over the years and have won them all. Africa, in what seems like a quick few years, is now the world power. Our place in history is restored. Now, other countries ask Africa for assistance and they model their countries after us and the way we do things.

One major difference to Africa, in my opinion, is that my dad has died. We think it was cancer, but we really don't know. Life is different without him, but I'm grateful for the time I had with him. My father taught me many things and one thing he taught me is how to live without him. That's what all of his life's lessons were about. He knew one day he'd be gone and he wanted to equip me as best as possible for that time. My dad is buried behind the pyramid he had built for us years ago. My dad is like Dr. Martin Luther King Jr. was in the 1960s. He is known all around Africa and is highly revered. Dr. Robinson is still alive. She spends her time educating Africans all around the continent. My dad's time machines are both safely tucked in separate locations that only I know. The slaves who built the structures that the time machines are hidden in had no idea what was being placed there to ensure they couldn't tell anyone. I don't know if I'll ever reveal the locations of the time machines or even visit them. I'm satisfied with the current state of things, but it's good to know that I have access to them if I need them. Africa is now the place where the entire world wants to be. We've accomplished the unthinkable and saved Africa and its people from being exploited by returning Africa to its rightful place. Africa now basks in the glory of being the reversed world power.

www.ingramcontent.com/pod-product-compliance
Lightning Source LLC
Chambersburg PA
CBHW070124260626
47160CB00004B/1613